T0065665

shoot the piano player

shoot the
piano player

david goodis

VINTAGE CRIME / **BLACK LIZARD**

vintage books • a division of random house, inc. • new york

First Vintage Crime / Black Lizard Edition, October 1990

Library of Congress Cataloging-in-Publication Data
Goodis, David, 1917–1967.
[Down there]
Shoot the piano player / by David Goodis — 1st Vintage crime / Black Lizard ed.
p.   cm. —(Vintage crime / Black Lizard)
"Originally published as Down there" — T.p. verso.
ISBN 0-679-73254-3
I S B N - 13: 978-0-679-73254-9
I. Title.   II. Series.
PS3513.0499S56   1990
813'.52—dc20   90-50255   CIP

146086900

shoot the piano player

There were no street lamps, no lights at all. It was a narrow street in the Port Richmond section of Philadelphia. From the nearby Delaware a cold wind came lancing in, telling all alley cats they'd better find a heated cellar. The late November gusts rattled against midnight-darkened windows, and stabbed at the eyes of the fallen man in the street.

The man was kneeling near the curb, breathing hard and spitting blood and wondering seriously if his skull was fractured. He'd been running blindly, his head down, so of course he hadn't seen the telephone pole. He'd crashed into it face first, bounced away and hit the cobblestones and wanted to call it a night.

But you can't do that, he told himself. You gotta get up and keep running.

He got up slowly, dizzily. There was a big lump on the left side of his head, his left eye and cheekbone were somewhat swollen, and the inside of his cheek was bleeding where he'd bitten it when he'd hit the pole. He thought of what his face must look like, and he managed to grin, saying to himself, You're doing fine, jim. You're really in great shape. But I think you'll make it, he decided, and then he was running again, suddenly running very fast as the headlights rounded a corner, the car picking up speed, the engine noise closing in on him.

The beam of the headlights showed him the entrance to an alley. He veered, went shooting into the alley, went down the alley and came out on another narrow street.

Maybe this is it, he thought. Maybe this is the street you want. No, your luck is running good but not that good, I think you'll hafta do more running before you find that street, before you see that lit-up sign, that drinking joint where Eddie works, that place called Harriet's Hut.

The man kept running. At the end of the block he turned, went on to the next street, peering through the darkness for any hint of the lit-up sign. You gotta get there, he told himself. You gotta get to Eddie before they get to you. But I wish I knew this neighborhood better. I wish it wasn't so cold and dark around here, it sure ain't no night for traveling on foot. Especially when you're running, he added. When you're running away from a very fast Buick with two professionals in it, two high-grade operators, really experts in their line.

He came to another intersection, looked down the street, and at the end of the street, there it was, the orange glow, the lit-up sign of the tavern on the corner. The sign was very old, separate bulbs instead of neon tubes. Some of the bulbs were missing, the letters unreadable. But enough of it remained so that any wanderer could see it was a place for drinking. It was Harriet's Hut.

The man moved slowly now, more or less staggering as he headed toward the saloon. His head was throbbing, his windslashed lungs were either frozen or on fire, he wasn't quite sure what it felt like. And worst of all, his legs were heavy and getting heavier, his knees were giving way. But he staggered on, closer, to the lit-up sign, and closer yet, and finally he was at the side entrance.

He opened the door and walked into Harriet's Hut. It was a fairly large place, high-ceilinged, and it was at least thirty years behind the times. There was no juke box, no television set. In places the wallpaper was loose and some of it was ripped away. The chairs and tables had lost their varnish, and the brass of the bar-rail had no shine at all. Above the mirror behind the bar there was a faded and partially torn photograph of a very young aviator wearing his helmet and smiling up at the sky. The photograph was captioned "Lucky Lindy." Near it there was another photograph that showed Dempsey crouched and moving in on a calm and technical Tunney. On the wall adjacent to the left side of the bar there was a framed painting of Kendrick, who'd been mayor of Philadelphia during the Sesqui-Centennial.

At the bar the Friday night crowd was jammed three-and-four-deep. Most of the drinkers wore work pants and heavy-soled work shoes. Some were very old, sitting in groups at the tables, their hair white and their faces wrinkled. But their hands didn't tremble as they lifted beer mugs and shot glasses. They could still lift a drink as well as any Hut regular, and they held their alcohol with a certain straight-seated dignity that gave them the appearance of venerable elders at a town meeting.

The place was really packed. All the tables were taken, and there wasn't a single empty chair for a leg-weary newcomer.

But the leg-weary man wasn't looking for a chair. He was looking for the piano. He could hear the music coming from the piano, but he couldn't see the instrument. A view-blurring fog of tobacco smoke and liquor fumes made everything vague, almost opaque. Or maybe it's me, he thought. Maybe I'm just about done in, and ready to keel over.

He moved. He went staggering past the tables, headed in the direction of the piano music. Nobody paid any attention to him, not even when he stumbled and went down. At twelve-twenty on a Friday night most patrons of Harriet's Hut were either booze-happy or booze-groggy. They were Port Richmond mill workers who'd labored hard all week. They came here to drink and drink some more, to forget all serious business, to ignore each and every problem of the too-real too-dry world beyond the walls of the Hut. They didn't even see the man who was pulling himself up very slowly from the sawdust on the floor, standing there with his bruised face and bleeding mouth, grinning and mumbling, "I can hear the music, all right. But where's the goddam piano?"

Then he was staggering again, bumping into a pile of high-stacked beer cases set up against a wall. It formed a sort of pyramid, and he groped his way along it, his hands feeling the cardboard of the beer cases until finally there was no more cardboard and he almost went down again. What kept him on his feet was the sight of the piano, specifically the sight of the pianist who sat there on the circular stool, slightly bent over, aiming a dim and faraway smile at nothing in particular.

The bruised-faced, leg-weary man, who was fairly tall

and very wide across the shoulders and had a thick mop of ruffled yellow hair, moved closer to the piano. He came up behind the musician and put a hand on his shoulder and said, "Hello, Eddie."

There was no response from the musician, not even a twitch of the shoulder on which the man's heavy hand applied more pressure. And the man thought, Like he's far away, he don't even feel it, he's all the way out there with his music, it's a crying shame you gotta bring him in, but that's the way it is, you got no choice.

"Eddie," the man said, louder now. "It's me, Eddie."

The music went on, the rhythm unbroken. It was a soft, easygoing rhythm, somewhat plaintive and dreamy, a stream of pleasant sound that seemed to be saying, Nothing matters.

"It's me," the man said, shaking the musician's shoulder. "It's Turley. Your brother Turley."

The musician went on making the music. Turley sighed and shook his head slowly. He thought, You can't reach this one. It's like he's in a cloud and nothing moves him.

But then the tune was ended. The musician turned slowly and looked at the man and said, "Hello, Turley."

"You're sure a cool proposition," Turley said. "You ain't seen me for six-seven years. You look at me as if I just came back from a walk around the block."

"You bump into something?" the musician inquired mildly, scanning the bruised face, the bloodstained mouth.

Just then a woman got up from a nearby table and made a beeline for a door marked *Girls*. Turley spotted the empty chair, grabbed it, pulled it toward the piano and sat down. A man at the table yelled, "Hey you, that chair is taken," and Turley said to the man, "Easy now, jim. Cantcha see I'm an invalid?" He turned to the musician and grinned again, saying, "Yeah, I bumped into something. The street was too dark and I hit a pole."

"Who you running from?"

"Not the law, if that's what you're thinking."

"I'm not thinking anything," the musician said. He was medium-sized, on the lean side, and in his early thirties. He sat there with no particular expression on his face.

He had a pleasant face. There were no deep lines, no

shadows. His eyes were a soft gray and he had a soft, relaxed mouth. His light-brown hair was loosely combed, very loosely, as though he combed it with his fingers. The shirt collar was open and there was no necktie. He wore a wrinkled, patched jacket and patched trousers. The clothes had a timeless look, indifferent to the calendar and the mens' fashion columns. The man's full name was Edward Webster Lynn and his sole occupation was here at the Hut where he played the piano six nights a week, between nine and two. His salary was thirty dollars, and with tips his weekly income was anywhere from thirty-five to forty. It more than paid for his requirements. He was unmarried, he didn't own a car, and he had no debts or obligations.

"Well, anyway," Turley was saying, "it ain't the law. If it was the law, I wouldn't be pulling you into it."

"Is that why you came here?" Eddie asked softly. "To pull me into something?"

Turley didn't reply. He turned his head slightly, looking away from the musician. Consternation clouded his face, as though he knew what he wanted to say but couldn't quite manage to say it.

"It's no go," Eddie said.

Turley let out a sigh. As it faded, the grin came back. "Well, anyway, how you doing?"

"I'm doing fine," Eddie said.

"No problems?"

"None at all. Everything's dandy."

"Including the finance?"

"I'm breaking even." Eddie shrugged, but his eyes narrowed slightly.

Turley sighed again.

Eddie said, "I'm sorry, Turl, it's strictly no dice."

"But listen—"

"No," Eddie said softly. "No matter what it is, you can't pull me into it."

"But Jesus Christ, the least you can do is—"

"How's the family?" Eddie asked.

"The family?" Turley was blinking. Then he picked up on it. "We're all in good shape. Mom and Dad are okay—"

"And Clifton?" Eddie said. "How's Clifton?" referring to the other brother, the oldest.

Turley's grin was suddenly wide. "Well, you know how it is with Clifton. He's still in there pitching—"

"Strikes?"

Turley didn't answer. The grin stayed, but it seemed to slacken just a little. Then presently he said, "You've been away a long time. We miss you."

Eddie shrugged.

"We really miss you," Turley said. "We always talk about you."

Eddie gazed past his brother. The far-off smile drifted across his lips. He didn't say anything.

"After all," Turley said, "you're one of the family. We never told you to leave. I mean you're always welcome at the house. What I mean is—"

"How'd you know where to find me?"

"Fact is, I didn't. Not at first. Then I remembered, that last letter we got, you mentioned the name of this place. I figured you'd still be here. Anyway, I hoped so. Well, today I was downtown and I looked up the address in the phone book—"

"Today?"

"I mean tonight. I mean—"

"You mean when things got tight you looked me up. Isn't that it?"

Turley blinked again. "Don't get riled."

"Who's riled?"

"You're plenty riled but you cover it up," Turley said. Then he had the grin working again. "I guess you learned that trick from living here in the city. All us country people, us South Jersey melon-eaters, we can't ever learn that caper. We always gotta show our hole card."

Eddie made no comment. He glanced idly at the keyboard, and hit a few notes.

"I got myself in a jam," Turley said.

Eddie went on playing. The notes were in the higher octaves, the fingers very light on the keyboard, making a cheery, babbling-brook sort of tune.

Turley shifted his position in the chair. He was glancing around, his eyes swiftly checking the front door, the side door, and the door leading to the rear exit.

"Wanna hear something pretty?" Eddie said. "Listen to this—"

Turley's hand came down on the fingers that were hitting the keys. Through the resulting discord, his voice came urgently, somewhat hoarsely. "You gotta help me, Eddie. I'm really in a tight spot. You can't turn me down."

"Can't get myself involved, either."

"Believe me, it won't get you involved. All I'm asking, lemme stay in your room until morning."

"You don't mean stay. You mean hide."

Again Turley sighed heavily. Then he nodded.

"From who?" Eddie asked.

"Two troublemakers."

"Really? You sure they made the trouble? Maybe you made it."

"No, they made it," Turley said. "They been giving me grief since early today."

"Get to it. What kind of grief?"

"Tracing me. They've been on my neck from the time I left Dock Street—"

"Dock Street?" Eddie frowned slightly. "What were you doing on Dock Street?"

"Well, I was—" Turley faltered, swallowed hard, then bypassed Dock Street and blurted, "Damn it all, I ain't askin' for the moon. All you gotta do is put me up for the night—"

"Hold it," Eddie said. "Let's get back to Dock Street."

"For Christ's sake—"

"And another thing," Eddie went on. "What're you doing here in Philadelphia?"

"Business."

"Like what?"

Turley didn't seem to hear the question. He took a deep breath. "Something went haywire. Next thing I know, I got these two on my neck. And then, what fixes me proper, I run clean outta folding money. It happens in a hash house on Delaware Avenue when some joker lifts my wallet. If it hadn't been for that, I coulda bought some transportation, at least a taxi to get past the city limits. As it was, all I had left was nickels and dimes, so every time I'm on a streetcar they're right behind me in a brand-new Buick. I tell you, it's been a mean Friday for me, jim. Of all the goddam days to get my pocket picked—"

"You still haven't told me anything."

"I'll give you the rundown later. Right now I'm pushed for time."

As Turley said it, he was turning his head to have another look at the door leading to the street. Absently he lifted his fingers to the battered left side of his face, and grimaced painfully. The grimace faded as the dizziness came again, and he weaved from side to side, as though the chair had wheels and was moving along a bumpy road. "Whatsa matter with the floor?" he mumbled, his eyes half closed now. "What kinda dump is this? Can't they even fix the floor? It won't even hold the chair straight."

He began to slide from the chair. Eddie grabbed his shoulders and steadied him.

"You'll be all right," Eddie said. "Just relax."

"Relax?" It came out vaguely. "Who wantsa relax?" Turley's arm flapped weakly to indicate the jam-packed bar and the crowded tables. "Look at the people having fun. Why can't I have some fun? Why can't I—"

It's bad, Eddie thought. It's worse than I figured it was. He's got some real damage upstairs. I think what we'll hafta do is—

"Whatsa matter with him?" a voice said.

Eddie looked up and saw the Hut's owner, Harriet. She was a very fat woman in her middle forties. She had peroxide-blonde hair, a huge, jutting bosom and tremendous hips. Despite the excess weight, she had a somewhat narrow waistline. Her face was on the Slavic side, the nose broad-based and moderately pugged, the eyes gray-blue with a certain level look that said, You deal with me, you deal straight. I got no time for two-bit sharpies, fast-hand slicksters, or any kind of leeches, fakers, and freebee artists. Get cute or cagey and you'll wind up buying new teeth.

Turley was slipping off the chair again. Harriet caught him as he sagged sideways. Her fat hands held him firmly under his armpits while she leaned closer to examine the lump on his head.

"He's sorta banged up," Eddie said. "He's really groggy. I think—"

"He ain't as groggy as he looks," Harriet cut in dryly. "If he don't stop what he's doing he's gonna get banged up more."

Turley had sent one arm around her hip, his hand sliding onto the extra-large, soft-solid bulge. She reached back, grabbed his wrist and flung his arm aside. "You're either wine-crazy, punch-crazy, or plain crazy," she informed him. "You try that again, you'll need a brace on your jaw. Now sit still while I have a look."

"I'll have a look too," Turley said, and while the fat woman bent over him to study his damaged skull, he made a serious study of her forty-four-inch bosom. Again his arm went around her hip, and again she flung it off. "You're askin' for it," she told him, hefting her big fist. "You really want it, don't you?"

Turley grinned past the fist. "I always do, blondie. Ain't no hour of the day when I don't."

"You think he needs a doctor?" Eddie asked.

"I'll settle for a big fat nurse," Turley babbled, the grin very loose, sort of idiotic. And then he looked around, as though trying to figure out where he was. "Hey, somebody tell me somethin'. I'd simply like to know—"

"What year it is?" Harriet said. "It's Nineteen fifty-six, and the city is Philadelphia."

"You'll hafta do better than that." Turley sat up straighter. "What I really wanna know is—" But the fog enveloped him and he sat there gazing vacantly past Harriet, past Eddie, his eyes glazing over.

Harriet and Eddie looked at him, then looked at each other. Eddie said, "Keeps up like this, he'll need a stretcher."

Harriet took another look at Turley. She made a final diagnosis, saying, "He'll be all right. I've seen them like that before. In the ring. A certain nerve gets hit and they lose all track of what's happening. Then first thing you know, they're back in stride, they're doing fine."

Eddie was only half convinced. "You really think he'll be okay?"

"Sure he will," Harriet said. "Just look at him. He's made

of rock. I know this kind. They take it and like it and come back for more."

"That's correct," Turley said solemnly. Without looking at Harriet, he reached out to shake her hand. Then he changed his mind and his hand strayed in another direction. Harriet shook her head in motherly disapproval. A wistful smile came onto her blunt features, a smile of understanding. She lowered her hand to Turley's head, her fingers in his mussed-up hair to muss it up some more, to let him know that Harriet's Hut was not as mean-hard as it looked, that it was a place where he could rest a while and pull himself together.

"You know him?" she said to Eddie. "Who is he?"

Before Eddie could answer, Turley was off on another fogbound ride, saying, "Look at that over there across the room. What's that?"

Harriet spoke soothingly, somewhat clinically. "What is it, johnny? Where?"

Turley's arm came up. He tried to point. It took considerable effort and finally he made it.

"You mean the waitress?" Harriet asked.

Turley couldn't answer. He had his eyes fastened on the face and body of the brunette on the other side of the room. She wore an apron and she carried a tray.

"You really like that?" Harriet asked. Again she mussed his hair. She threw a wink at Eddie.

"Like it?" Turley was saying. "I been lookin' all over for something in that line. That's my kind of material. I wanna get to meet that. What's her name?"

"Lena."

"She's something," Turley said. He rubbed his hands. "She's really something."

"So what are your plans?" Harriet asked quietly, as though she meant it seriously.

"Four bits is all I need." Turley's tone was flat and technical.

"A drink for me and a drink for her. And that'll get things going."

"Sure as hell it will," Harriet said, saying it more to herself and with genuine seriousness, her eyes aimed now across the crowded Hut, focused on the waitress. And then, to Turley, "You think you got lumps now, you'll get real lumps if you make a pass at that."

She looked at Eddie, waiting for some comment. Eddie had pulled away from it. He'd turned to face the keyboard. His face showed the dim and far-off smile and nothing more.

Turley stood up to get a better look. "What's her name again?"

"Lena."

"So that's Lena," he said, his lips moving slowly.

"That's sheer aggravation," Harriet said. "Do yourself a favor. Sit down. Stop looking."

He sat down, but he went on looking. "How come it's aggravation?" he wanted to know. "You mean it ain't for sale or rent?"

"It ain't available, period."

"Married?"

"No, she ain't married," Harriet said very slowly. Her eyes were riveted on the waitress.

"Then what's the setup?" Turley insisted on knowing. "She hooked up with someone?"

"No," Harriet said. "She's strictly solo. She wants no part of any man. A man moves in too close, he gets it from the hatpin."

"Hatpin?"

"She's got it stuck there in that apron. Some hungry rooster gets too hungry, she jabs him where it really hurts."

Turley snorted. "Is that all?"

"No," Harriet said. "That ain't all. The hatpin is only the beginning. Next thing the poor devil knows, he's getting it from the bouncer. That's her number-one protection, the bouncer."

"Who's the bouncer? Where is he?"

Harriet pointed toward the bar.

Turley peered through the clouds of tobacco smoke. "Hey, wait now, I've seen a picture somewhere. In the papers—"

"On the sports page, it musta been." Harriet's voice was queerly thick. "They had him tagged as the Harleyville Hugger."

"That's right," Turley said. "The Hugger. I remember. Sure, I remember now."

Harriet looked at Turley. She said, "You really do?"

"Sure," Turley said. "I'm a wrestling fan from way back. Never had the cabbage to buy tickets, but I followed it in the papers." He peered again toward the bar. "That's him, all right. That's the Harleyville Hugger."

"And it wasn't no fake when he hugged them, either," Harriet said. "You know anything about the game, you know what a bear hug can do. I mean the real article. He'd get them in a bear hug, they were finished." And then, significantly, "He still knows how."

Turley snorted again. He looked from the bouncer to the waitress and back to the bouncer. "That big-bellied slob?"

"He still has it, regardless. He's a crushing machine."

"He couldn't crush my little finger," Turley said. "I'd hook one short left to that paunch and he'd scream for help. Why, he ain't nothing but a worn-out—"

Turley was vaguely aware that he'd lost his listener. He turned and looked and Harriet wasn't there. She was walking toward the stairway near the bar. She mounted the stairway, ascending very slowly, her head lowered.

"Whatsa matter with her?" Turley asked Eddie. "She got a headache?"

Eddie was half turned away from the keyboard, watching Harriet as she climbed the stairs. Then he turned fully to the keyboard and hit a few idle notes. His voice came softly through the music. "I guess you could call it a headache. She got a problem with the bouncer. He has it bad for the waitress—"

"Me, too," Turley grinned.

Eddie went on hitting the notes, working in some chords, building a melody. "With the bouncer it's real bad. And Harriet knows."

"So what?" Turley frowned vaguely. "What's the bouncer to her?"

"They live together," Eddie said. "He's her common-law husband."

Then Turley sagged again, falling forward, bumping into Eddie, holding on to him for support. Eddie went on playing the piano. Turley let go and sat back in the chair. He was waiting for Eddie to turn around and look at him. And finally Eddie stopped playing and turned and looked. He saw the grin on Turley's face. Again it was the idiotic eyes-glazed grin.

"You want a drink?" Eddie asked. "Maybe you could use a drink."

"I don't need no drink." Turley swayed from side to side. "Tell you what I need. I need some information. Wanna be straightened out on something. You wanna help me on that?"

"Help you on what?" Eddie murmured. "What is it you wanna know?"

Turley shut his eyes tightly. He opened them, shut them, opened them again. He saw Eddie sitting there. He said, "What you doin' here?"

Eddie shrugged.

Turley had his own answer. "I'll tell you what you're doing. You're wasting away—"

"All right," Eddie said gently. "All right—"

"It ain't all right," Turley said. And then the disjointed phrases spilled from the muddled brain. "Sits there at a second-hand piano. Wearing rags. When what you should be wearing is a full-dress suit. With one of them ties, the really fancy duds. And it should be a grand piano, a great big shiny grand piano, one of them Steinbergs, god-damn it, with every seat taken in the concert hall. That's where you should be, and what I want to know is—why ain't you there?"

"You really need a bracer, Turl. You're away off the groove."

"Don't study my condition, jim. Study your own. Why ain't you there in that concert hall?"

Eddie shrugged and let it slide past.

But Turley banged his hands against his knees. "Why ain't you there?"

"Because I'm here," Eddie said. "I can't be two places at once."

It didn't get across. "Don't make sense," Turley blab-bered. "Just don't make sense at all. A knockout of a dame and she ain't got no boy friend. A Piano man as good as they come and he don't make enough to buy new shoes."

Eddie laughed.

"It ain't comical," Turley said. "It's a screwed-up state of affairs." He spoke to some invisible third party, pointing a finger at the placid-faced musician. "Here he sits at this wreck of a piano, in this dirty old crummy old joint that oughtta be inspected by the fire marshal, or anyway by the Board of Health. Look at the floor, they still use sawdust on the god-dam floor—" He cupped his hands to his mouth and called, "At least buy some new chairs, for Christ's sake—" Then referring again to the soft-eyed musician, "Sits here, night after night. Sits here wasting away in the bush leagues when he oughtta be way up there in the majors, way up at the top cause he's got the stuff, he's got it in them ten fingers. He's a star, I tell you, he's the star of them all—"

"Easy, Turl—"

Turley was feeling it deep. He stood up, shouting again, "It oughtta be a grand piano, with candlesticks like that other cat has. Where's the candlesticks? Whatsa matter here? You cheap or somethin'? You can't afford no candlesticks?"

"Aaah, close yer head," some nearby beerguzzler offered.

Turley didn't hear the heckler. He went on shouting, tears streaming down his rough-featured face. The cuts in his mouth had opened again and the blood was trickling from his lips. "And there's something wrong somewhere," he proclaimed to the audience that had no idea who he was or what he was talking about, "—like anyone knows that two and two adds up to four but this adds up to minus three. It just ain't right and it calls for some kind of action—"

"You really want action?" a voice inquired pleasantly.

It was the voice of the bouncer, formerly known as the Harleyville Hugger, known now in the Hut by his real name, Wally Plyne, although certain admirers still insisted it was Hugger. He stood there, five feet nine and weighing two-twenty. There was very little hair on his head, and what remained was clipped short, fuzzy. His left ear was somewhat out of shape, and his nose was a wreck, fractured so many times that now it was hardly a nose at all. It was more like a blob of putty flattened onto the rough-grained face. In Plyne's mouth there was considerable bridgework, and ribboning down from his chin and toward the collarbone was a poorly stitched scar, obviously an emergency job performed by some intern. Plyne was not pleased with the scar. He wore his shirt collar buttoned high to conceal it as much as possible. He was extremely sensitive about his battered face, and when anyone looked at him too closely he'd stiffen and his neck would swell and redden. His eyes would plead with the looker not to laugh. There'd been times when certain lookers had ignored the plea, and the next thing they knew, their ribs were fractured and they had severe internal injuries. At Harriet's Hut the first law of self-preservation was never laugh at the bouncer.

The bouncer was forty-three years old.

He stood there looking down at Turley. He was waiting for an answer. Turley looked up at him and said, "Why you buttin' in? Cantcha see I'm talkin'?"

"You're talking too loud," Plyne said. His tone remained pleasant, almost sympathetic. He was looking at the tears rolling down Turley's cheeks.

"If I don't talk loud they won't hear me," Turley said. "I want them to hear me."

"They got other things to do," Plyne said patiently. "They're drinkin' and they don't wanna be bothered."

"That's what's wrong," Turley sobbed. "Nobody wantsa be bothered."

Plyne took a deep breath. He said to Turley, "Now look, whoever messed up your face like that, you go ahead and hit him back. But not here. This here's a quiet place of business—"

"What you sellin' me?" Turley blinked the tears away, his tone changing to a growl. "Who asked you to be sorry for my goddam face? It's my face. The lumps are mine, the cuts are mine. You better worry about your own damn face."

"Worry?" Plyne was giving careful thought to the remark. "How you mean that?"

Turley's eyes and lips started a grin, his mouth started a reply. Before the grin could widen, before the words could come, Eddie moved in quickly, saying to Plyne, "He didn't mean anything, Wally. Cantcha see he's all mixed up?"

"You stay out of this," Plyne said, not looking at Eddie. He was studying Turley's face, waiting for the grin to go away.

The grin remained. At nearby tables there was a waiting quiet. The quiet spread to other tables, then to all the tables, and then to the crowded bar. They were all staring at the big man who stood there grinning at Plyne.

"Get it off," Plyne told Turley. "Get it off your face."

Turley widened the grin.

Plyne took another deep breath. Something came into his eyes, a kind of dull glow. Eddie saw it and knew what it meant. He was up from the piano stool, saying to Plyne, "Don't, Wally. He's sick."

"Who's sick?" Turley challenged. "I'm in grade-A shape. I'm ready for—"

"He's ready for a brain examination," Eddie said to Plyne, to the staring audience. "He ran into a pole and banged his head. Look at that bump. If it ain't a fracture it's maybe a concussion."

"Call for an ambulance," someone directed.

"Lookit, he's bleeding from the mouth," another voice put in. "Could be that's from the busted head."

Plyne blinked a few times. The glow faded from his eyes.

Turley went on grinning. But now the grin wasn't aimed at Plyne or anyone or anything else. Again it was the idiotic grin.

Plyne looked at Eddie. "You know him?"

Eddie shrugged. "Sort of."

"Who is he?"

Another shrug. "I'll take him outside. Let him get some air—"

Plyne's thick fingers closed on Eddie's sleeve. "I asked you something. Who is he?"

"You hear the man?" It was Turley again, coming out of the brain-battered fog. "The man says he wantsa know. I think he's got a point there."

"Then you tell me," Plyne said to Turley. He stepped closer, peering into the glazed eyes. "Maybe you don't need an ambulance, after all. Maybe you ain't really hurt that bad. Can you tell me who you are?"

"Brother."

"Whose brother?"

"His." Turley pointed to Eddie.

"I didn't know he had a brother," Plyne said.

"Well, that's the way it goes." Turley spoke to all the nearby tables. "You learn something new every day."

"I'm willing to learn," Plyne said. And then, as though Eddie wasn't there, "He never talks about himself. There's a lota things about him I don't know."

"You don't?" Turley had the grin again. "How long has he worked here?"

"Three years."

"That's a long time," Turley said. "You sure oughtta have him down pat by now.

"Nobody's got him down pat. Only thing we know for sure, he plays the piano."

"You pay him wages?"

"Sure we pay him wages."

"To do what?"

"Play the piano."

"And what else?"

"Just that," Plyne said. "We pay him to play the piano, that's all."

"You mean you don't pay him wages to talk about himself?"

Plyne tightened his lips. He didn't reply.

Turley moved in closer. "You want it all for free, don't you? But the thing is, you can't get it for free. You wanna learn about a person, it costs you. And the more you learn, the more it costs. Like digging a well, the deeper you go, the more expenses you got. And sometimes it's a helluva lot more than you can afford."

"What you getting at?" Plyne was frowning now. He turned his head to look at the piano man. He saw the care-free smile and it bothered him, it caused his frown to darken. There was only a moment of that, and then he looked again at Turley. He got rid of the frown and said, "All right, never mind. This talk means nothing. It's jabber, and you're punchy, and I got other things to do. I can't stay here wasting time with you."

The bouncer walked away. The audience at the bar and the tables went back to drinking. Turley and Eddie were seated now, Eddie facing the keyboard, hitting a few chords and starting a tune. It was a placid, soft-sweet tune and the dreamy sounds brought a dreamy smile to

Turley's lips. "That's nice," Turley whispered. "That's really nice."

The music went on and Turley nodded slowly, unaware that he was nodding. As his head came up, and started to go down again, he saw the front door open.

Two men came in.

That's them," Turley said.

Eddie went on making the music.

"That's them, all right," Turley said matter-of-factly.

The door closed behind the two men and they stood there turning their heads very slowly, looking from crowded tables to crowded bar, back to the tables, to the bar again, looking everywhere.

Then they spotted Turley. They started forward.

"Here they come," Turley said, still matter-of-factly. "Look at them."

Eddie's eyes stayed on the keyboard. He had his mind on the keyboard. The warm-cool music flowed on and now it was saying to Turley, It's your problem, entirely yours, keep me out of it.

The two men came closer. They moved slowly. The tables were close-packed, blocking their path. They were trying to move faster, to force their way through.

"Here they come," Turley said. "They're really coming now."

Don't look, Eddie said to himself. You take one look and that'll do it, that'll pull you into it. You don't want that, you're here to play the piano, period. But what's this? What's happening? There ain't no music now, your fingers are off the keyboard.

He turned his head and looked and saw the two men coming closer.

They were well-dressed men. The one in front was short and very thin, wearing a pearl-gray felt hat and a white silk muffler and a single-breasted, dark blue overcoat. The man behind him was thin, too, but much taller. He wore a hat of darker gray, a black-and-silver striped muffler, and his overcoat was a dark gray six-button-benny.

Now they were halfway across the room. There was more space here between the tables. They were coming faster.

Eddie jabbed stiffened fingers into Turley's ribs. "Don't sit there. Get up and go."

"Go where?" And there it was again, the idiotic grin.

"Side door," Eddie hissed at him, gave him another finger-stiffened jab, harder this time.

"Hey, quit that," Turley said. "That hurts."

"Does it?" Another jab made it really hurt, pulled the grin off Turley's face, pulled his rump off the chair. Then Turley was using his legs, going past the stacked pyramid of beer cases, walking faster and faster and finally lunging toward the side door.

The two men took a short cut, going diagonally away from the tables. They were running now, streaking to intercept Turley. It looked as though they had it made.

Then Eddie was up from the piano stool, seeing Turley aiming at the side door some fifteen feet away. The two men were closing in on Turley. They'd pivoted off the diagonal path and now they ran parallel to the pyramid of beer cases. Eddie made a short rush that took him into the high-stacked pile of bottle-filled cardboard boxes. He gave the pile a shoulder bump and a box came down and then another box, and more boxes. It caused a traffic jam as the two men collided with the fallen beer cases, tripped over the cardboard hurdles, went down and got up and tripped again. While that happened, Turley opened the side door and ran out.

Some nine beer cases had fallen off the stacked pyramid and several of the bottles had come loose to hit the floor and break. The two men were working hard to get past the blockade of cardboard boxes and broken bottles. One of them, the shorter one, was turning his head to catch a glimpse of whatever funnyman had caused this fiasco. He saw Eddie standing there near the partially crumbled pyramid. Eddie shrugged and lifted his arms in a sheepish gesture, as though to say, An accident, I just bumped into it, that's all. The short thin man didn't say anything. There wasn't time for a remark.

Eddie went back to the piano. He sat down and started to play. He hit a few soft chords, the dim and far-off smile drifting onto his lips while the two thin well-dressed men finally made it to the side door. Through the soft sound of the music he heard the hard sound of the door slamming shut behind them.

He went on playing. There were no wrong notes, no breaks in the rhythm, but he was thinking of Turley, seeing the two men going after Turley along the too-dark streets in the too-cold stillness out there that might be broken any moment now by the sound of a shot.

But I don't think so, he told himself. They didn't have that look, as though they were gunning for meat. It was more of a bargaining look, like all they want is to sit down with Turley and talk some business.

What kind of business? Well, sure, you know what kind. It's something on the shady side. He said it was Clifton's transaction and that puts it on the shady side, with Turl stooging for Clifton like he's always done. So whatever it is, they're in a jam again, your two dear brothers. It's a first-class talent they have for getting into jams, getting out, and getting in again. You think they'll get out this time? Well, we hope so. We really hope so. We wish them luck, and that about says it. So what you do now is get off the trolley. It ain't your ride and you're away from it.

A shadow fell across the keyboard. He tried not to see it, but it was there and it stayed there. He turned his head sideways and saw the bulky legs, the barrel torso and the mashed-nosed face of the bouncer.

He went on playing.

"That's pretty," Plyne said.

Eddie nodded his thanks.

"It's very pretty," Plyne said. "But it just ain't pretty enough. I don't wanna hear any more."

Eddie stopped playing. His arms came down limply at his sides. He sat there and waited.

"Tell me something," the bouncer said. "What is it with you?"

Eddie shrugged.

Plyne took a deep breath. "God damn it," he said to no

one in particular. "I've known this party for three years now and I hardly know him at all."

Eddie's soft smile was aimed at the keyboard. He tapped out a few idle notes in the middle octaves.

"That's all you'll ever get from him," Plyne said to invisible listeners. "That same no-score routine. No matter what comes up, it's always I-don't-know-from-nothing."

Eddie's fingers stayed there in the middle octaves.

The bouncer's manner changed. His voice was hard. "I told you to stop playing."

The music stopped. Eddie went on looking at the keyboard. He said, "What is it, Wally? What is it bothers you?"

"You really wanna know?" Plyne said it slowly, as though he'd scored a point. "All right, take a look." His arm stretched out, the forefinger rigid and aiming at the littered floor, the overturned cardboard boxes, the bottles, the scattered glass and the spilled beer foaming on the splintered floor boards.

Eddie shrugged again. "I'll clean it up," he said, and started to rise from the piano stool. Plyne pushed him back onto it.

"Tell me," Plyne said, and pointed again at the beer-stained floor. "What's the deal on that?"

"Deal?" The piano man seemed bewildered. "No deal at all. It was an accident. I didn't see where I was going, and I bumped into—"

But it was no use going on. The bouncer wasn't buying it. "Wanna bet?" the bouncer asked mildly. "Wanna bet it wasn't no accident?"

Eddie didn't reply.

"You won't tell me, I'll tell you," Plyne said. "A tagteam play, that's what it was."

"Could be." Eddie gave a very slight shrug. "I might have done it without thinking, I mean sort of unconsciouslike. I'm really not sure—"

"Not much you ain't." Plyne showed a thick wet smile that widened gradually. "You handled that stunt like you'd planned it on paper. The timing was perfect."

Eddie blinked several times. He told himself to stop it. He said to himself, Something is happening here and you better check it before it goes further.

But there was no way to check it. The bouncer was saying, "First time I ever saw you pull that kind of caper. In all the years you been here, you never butted in, not once. No matter what the issue was, no matter who was in it. So how come you butted in tonight?"

Another slight shrug, and the words coming softly, "I might have figured he could use some help, like I said, I'm not really sure. Or, on the other hand, you see someone in a jam, you remind yourself he's a close relative—I don't know, it's something along those lines."

Plyne's face twisted in a sort of disgusted grimace, as though he knew there was no use digging any deeper. He turned and started away from the piano.

Then something stopped him and caused him to turn and come back. He leaned against the side of the piano. For some moments he said nothing, just listened to the music, his brow creased slightly in a moderately thoughtful frown. Then, quite casually, he moved his heavy hand, brushing Eddie's fingers away from the keyboard.

Eddie looked up, waiting.

"Gimme some more on this transaction," the bouncer said.

"Like what?"

"Them two men you stalled with the beer cases. What's the wire on them?"

"I don't know," Eddie said.

"You don't know why they were chasing him?"

"Ain't got the least idea."

"Come on, come on."

"I can't tell you, Wally. I just don't know."

"You expect me to buy that?"

Eddie shrugged and didn't reply.

"All right," Plyne said. "We'll try it from another angle. This brother of yours. What's his line?"

"Don't know that either. Ain't seen him for years. Last I knew, he was working on Dock Street."

"Doing what?"

"Longshoreman."

"You don't know what he's doing now?"

"If I knew, I'd tell you."

"Yeah, sure." Plyne was folding his thick arms high on his chest. "Spill," he said. "Come on, spill."

Eddie smiled amiably at the bouncer. "What's all this courtroom action?" And then, the smile widening, "You going to law school, Wally? You practicing on me?"

"It ain't like that," Plyne said. He was stumped for a moment. "It's just that I wanna be sure, that's all. I mean—well, the thing of it is, I'm general manager here. Whatever happens in the Hut, I'm sorta responsible. You know that."

Eddie nodded, his eyebrows up. "That's a point."

"You're damn right it is," the bouncer pressed his advantage. "I gotta make sure this place keeps its license. It's a legitimate place of business. If I got anything to say, it's gonna stay legitimate."

"You're absolutely right," Eddie said.

"I'm glad you know it." Plyne's eyes were narrowed again. "Another thing you'd better know, I got more brains than you think. Can't play no music or write poems or anything like that, but sure as hell I can add up a score. Like with this brother of yours and them two engineers who wanted him for more than just a friendly chat."

"That adds," Eddie said.

"It adds perfect," Plyne approved his own arithmetic. "And I'll add it some more. I'll give it to you right down the line. He mighta been a longshoreman then, but it's a cinch he's switched jobs. He's lookin' for a higher income now. Whatever work he's doing, there's heavy cash involved—"

Eddie was puzzled. He was saying to himself, The dumber you play it, the better.

"Them two engineers," the bouncer was saying, "they weren't no small-timers. I gandered the way they were dressed. Them overcoats were hand-stitched; I know that custom quality when I see it. So we take it from there, we do it with arrows—"

"With what?"

"With arrows," Plyne said, his finger tracing an arrowline on the side of the piano. "From them to your brother. From your brother to you."

"Me?" Eddie laughed lightly. "You're not adding it now. You're stretching it."

"But not too far," Plyne said. "Because it's more than just possible. Because there ain't nothing wrong with my peepers. I seen your brother sitting here and giving you that sales talk. It's like he wants you in on the deal, whatever it is—"

Eddie was laughing again.

"What's funny?" Plyne asked.

Eddie went on laughing. It wasn't loud laughter, but it was real. He was trying to hold it back and he couldn't.

"Is it me?" Plyne spoke very quietly. "You laughing at me?"

"At myself," Eddie managed to say through the laughter. "I got a gilt-framed picture of the setup. The big deal, with me the key man, that final arrow pointing at me. You must be kidding, Wally. Just take a look and see for yourself. Look at the key man."

Plyne looked, seeing the thirty-a-week musician who sat there at the battered piano, the soft-eyed, soft-mouthed nobody whose ambitions and goals aimed at exactly zero, who'd been working here three years without asking or even hinting for a raise. Who never grumbled when the tips were stingy, or griped about anything, for that matter, not even when ordered to help with the chairs and tables at closing time, to sweep the floor, to take out the trash.

Plyne's eyes focused on him and took him in. Three years, and aside from the music he made, his presence at the Hut meant nothing. It was almost as though he wasn't there and the piano was playing all by itself. Regardless of the action at the tables or the bar, the piano man was out of it, not even an observer. He had his back turned and his eyes on the keyboard, content to draw his pauper's wages and wear pauper's rags. A gutless wonder, Plyne decided, fascinated with this living example of absolute neutrality. Even the smile was something neutral. It was never aimed at a woman. It was aimed very far out there beyond all tangible targets, really far out there beyond the leftfield bleachers. So where does that take it? Plyne asked himself. And of course there was no answer, not even the slightest clue.

But even so, he made a final effort. He squinted hard at the piano man, and said, "Tell me one thing. Where'd you come from?"

"I was born," Eddie said.

The bouncer thought it over for some moments. Then, "Thanks for the tipoff. I had it figured you came from a cloud."

Eddie laughed softly. Plyne was walking away, going toward the bar. At the bar the dark-haired waitress was arranging shot glasses on a tray. Plyne approached her, hesitated, then came in close and said something to her. She didn't reply. She didn't even look at him. She picked up the tray and headed for one of the tables. Plyne stood motionless, staring at her, his mouth tight, his teeth biting hard at the inside of his lip.

The soft-easy music came drifting from the piano.

It was twenty minutes later and the last nightcapper had been ushered out. The bartender was cleaning the last of the glasses, and the bouncer had gone upstairs to bed. The waitress had her overcoat on and was lighting a cigarette as she leaned back against the wall and watched Eddie, who was sweeping the floor.

He finished sweeping, emptied the dust-pan, put the broom away, and took his overcoat off the hanger near the piano. It was a very old overcoat. The collar was torn and two buttons were missing. He didn't have a hat.

The waitress watched him as he walked toward the front door. He turned his head to smile at the bartender and say good night. And then, to the waitress, "See you, Lena."

"Wait," she said, moving toward him as he opened the front door.

He stood there smiling somewhat questioningly. In the four months she'd been working here, they'd never exchanged more than a friendly hello or good night. Never anything much more than that.

Now she was saying, "Can you spare six bits?"

"Sure." Without hesitation he reached into his pants pocket. But the questioning look remained. It even deepened just a little.

"I'm sorta stuck tonight," the waitress explained. "When Harriet pays me tomorrow, you'll get it back."

"No hurry," he said, giving her two quarters, two dimes and a nickel.

"It goes for a meal," Lena explained further, putting the coins into her purse. "I figured Harriet would cook me something, but she went to bed early, and I didn't want to bother her."

"Yeah, I saw her going upstairs," Eddie said. He paused a moment. "I guess she was tired."

"Well, she works hard," Lena said. She took a final puff at the cigarette and tossed it into a cuspidor. "I wonder how she does it. All that weight. I bet she's over two hundred."

"Way over," Eddie said. "But she carries it nice. It's packed in solid."

"Too much of it. She loses a little, she'll feel better."

"She feels all right."

Lena shrugged. She didn't say anything.

Eddie opened the door and stepped aside. She went out, and he followed her. She started across the pavement and he said, "See you tomorrow," and she stopped and turned and faced him. She said, "I think six bits is more than I need. A half is enough," and started to open her purse.

He said, "No, that's all right." But she came toward him, extending the quarter, saying, "At John's I can get a platter for forty. Another dime for coffee and that does it."

He waved away the silver quarter. He said, "You might want a piece of cake or something."

She came closer. "Go on, take it," pushing the coin toward him.

He grinned. "High finance."

"Will you please take it?"

"Who needs it? I won't starve."

"You sure you can spare it?" Her head was slanted, her eyes searching his face.

He went on grinning. "Quit worrying. I won't run short."

"Yeah, I know." She went on searching his face. "Your wallet gets low, you just pick up the phone and call your broker. Who's your broker?"

"It's a big firm on Wall Street. I fly to New York twice a week. Just to have a look at the board."

"When'd you eat last?"

He shrugged. "I had a sandwich—"

"When?"

"I don't know. Around four-thirty, maybe."

"Nothing in between?" And then, not waiting for an answer, "Come on, walk me to John's. You'll have something."

"But—"

"Come on, will you?" She took his arm and pulled him along. "You wanna live, you gotta eat."

It occurred to him that he was really hungry and he could use a bowl of soup and a hot platter. The wet-cold wind was getting through his thin coat and biting into him. The thought of hot food was pleasant. Then another thought came and he winced slightly. He had exactly twelve cents in his pocket.

He shrugged and went on walking with Lena. He decided to settle for a cup of coffee. At least the coffee would warm him up. But you really oughtta have something to eat, he told himself. How come you didn't eat tonight? You always grab a bite at the food counter at the Hut around twelve-thirty. But not tonight. You had nothing tonight. How come you forgot to fill your belly?

Then he remembered. That business with Turley, he told himself. You were busy with Turley and you forgot to eat.

I wonder if Turley made it or not. I wonder if he got away. He knows how to move around and he can take care of himself. Yes, I'd say the chances are he made it. You really think so? He was handicapped, you know. It's a cinch he wasn't in condition to play hare-and-hounds with him the hare. Well, what are you gonna do? You can't do anything. I wish you'd drop it.

And another thing. What is it with this one here, this waitress? What bothers her? You know there's something bothering her. You caught the slightest hint of it when she talked about Harriet. She was sorta fishing then, she had the line out. Well sure, that's what it is. She's worried about Harriet and the bouncer and their domestic difficulties, because the bouncer's got his eyes on someone else these days—this waitress here. Well, it ain't her fault. Only thing she offers Plyne is an ice-cold look whenever he tries to move in. So let him keep trying. What do you care? Say, you wanna do me a favor? Get outta my hair, you're bugging me.

But just then a queer idea came into his brain, a downright silly notion. He couldn't understand why it was there. He was wondering how tall the waitress was, whether she was taller than he was. He tried to discard the thought, but it stayed there. It nudged him, shoved him, and finally caused him to turn his head and look at her.

He had to look down a little. He was a few inches taller than the waitress. He estimated she stood about five-six in semi-high heels. So what? he asked himself, but he went on looking as they crossed a narrow street and passed under a street lamp. The coat she wore fitted rather tightly and it brought out the lines of her body. She was highwaisted and with her slimness and her certain way of walking, it made her look taller. I guess that's it, he thought. I was just curious about it, that's all.

But he went on looking. He didn't know why he was looking. The glow from the street lamp spread out and lighted her face and he saw her profiled features that wouldn't make her a cover girl or a model for cosmetic ads, she didn't have that kind of face. Except for the skin. Her skin was clear and it had the kind of texture guaranteed in cosmetic ads, but this didn't come from cosmetics. This was from inside, and he thought, Probably she's got a good stomach, or a good set of glands, it's something along that line. There's nothing fragile about this one. That ain't a fragile nose or mouth or chin, and yet it's female, more female than them fragile-pretty types who look more like ornaments than girls. All in all, I'd say this one could give them cards and spades and still come out ahead. No wonder the bouncer tries to move in. No wonder all the roosters at the bar are always looking twice when she winks past. And still she ain't interested just in anything wears pants.

It's as though she's all finished with that. Maybe something happened that made her say, That does it, that ends it. But now you're guessing. How come you're guessing? Next thing, you'll want to know how old she is. And merely incidentally, how old you think she is? I'd say around twenty-seven. Should we ask her? If you do, she'll ask you why you want to know. And all you can say is, I just wondered. All right, stop wondering. It ain't as if you're interested. You know you're not interested.

Then what is it? What put you on this line of thinking? You oughtta get off it, it's like a road with too many turns and first thing you know, you just don't know where you are. But why is it she never has much to say? And hardly ever smiles?

Come to think of it, she's strictly on the solemn side. Not dreary, really. It's just that she's serious-solemn, and yet you've seen her laugh, she'll laugh at something that's comical. That is, when it's really comical.

She was laughing now. She was looking at him and quietly laughing.

"What is it?" he asked.

"Like Charlie Chaplin," she said.

"Like who?"

"Charlie Chaplin. In them silent movies he used to make. When something puzzled him and he wanted to ask about it and couldn't find the words, he'd get a dumb look on his face. You hid it perfect just then."

"Did I?"

She nodded. Then she stopped laughing. She said, "What was it? What puzzled you?"

He smiled dimly. "If we're gonna get to John's, we oughtta keep walkin."

She didn't say anything. They went on walking, turning a corner and coming onto a rutted pavement that bordered a cobblestoned street.

They covered another block and on the corner there was a rectangular structure that had once been a trolley car and was now an eatery that stayed open all night. Some of the windows were cracked, much of the paint was scraped off, and the entrance door slanted on loose hinges. Above the entrance door a sign read, Best Food in Port Richmond— John's. They went in and started toward the counter and for some reason she pulled him away from the counter and into a booth. As they sat down he saw she was looking past him, her eyes aimed at the far end of the counter. Her face was expressionless. He knew who it was down there. He knew also why she'd talked him into walking with her when they'd left the Hut. She hadn't wanted him to walk alone. She'd seen his maneuver with the beer cases when the two men had made their try for Turley, and all that talk about you-gotta-eat was merely so that he shouldn't be on the street alone.

Very considerate of her, he thought. He smiled at her to hide his annoyance. But then it amused him, and he thought, She wants to play nursemaid, let her play nursemaid.

There weren't many people in the diner. He counted four at this section of the counter, and two couples in other booths. Behind the counter the short, chunky Greek named John was breaking eggs above the grill. So with John it comes to nine, he thought. We got nine witnesses in case they try something. I don't think they will. You had a good look at them in the Hut. They didn't look like dunces. No, they won't try anything now.

John served four fried eggs to a fat man at the counter, came out from behind the counter and went over to the booth. The waitress ordered roast pork and mashed potatoes and said she wanted an extra roll. He asked for a cup of coffee with cream. She said, "That all you gonna have?" He nodded and she said, "You know you're hungry. Order something."

He shook his head. John walked away from the booth. They sat there, not saying anything. He hummed a tune and lightly drummed his fingers on the tabletop.

Then she said, "You loaned me seventy-five cents. What you got left for yourself?"

"I'm really not hungry."

"Not much. Come on, tell me. How much change you got?"

He put his hand in his pants pockets "I hate to break this fifty-dollar bill."

"Now, listen—"

"Forget it," he cut in mildly. Then, his thumb flicking backward, "They still there?"

"Who?"

"You know who."

She looked past him, past the side of the booth, her eyes checking the far end of the counter. Then she looked at him and nodded slowly. She said, "It's my fault. I didn't use my head. I didn't stop to think they might be here—"

"What're they doing now? They still eating?"

"They're finished. They're just sitting there. Smoking."

"Looking?"

"Not at us. They were looking this way a minute ago. I don't think it meant anything. They can't see you."

"Then I guess it's all right," he said. He grinned.

She grinned back at him. "Sure, it's nothing to worry about. Even if they see you, they won't do anything."

"I know they won't." And then, widening the grin, "You won't let them."

"Me?" Her grin faded. She frowned slightly. "What can I do?"

"I guess you can do something." Then, breezily, "You could hold them off while I cut out."

"Is that a joke? Whatcha think I am, Joan of Arc?"

"Well, now that you mention it—"

"Lemme tell you something," she interrupted. "I don't know what's happening between you and them two and I don't care. Whatever it is, I want no part of it. That clear?"

"Sure." And then, with a slight shrug, "If that's the way you really feel about it."

"I said so, didn't I?"

"Yeah. You said so."

"What's that supposed to mean?" Her head was slanted and she was giving him a look. "You think I don't mean what I say?"

He shrugged again. "I don't think anything. You're doing all the arguing."

John arrived with the tray, served the platter and the coffee, figured the price with his fingers and said sixty-five cents. Eddie took the dime and two pennies from his pocket and put the coins on the table. She pushed the coins aside and gave John the seventy-five cents. Eddie smiled at John and pointed to the twelve cents on the table. John said thanks, picked up the coins and went back to the counter. Eddie leaned low over the steaming black coffee, blew on it to cool it, and began sipping it. There was no sound from the other side of the table. He sensed that she wasn't eating, but was just sitting watching him. He didn't look up. He went on sipping the coffee. It was very hot and he sipped it slowly. Then he heard the noise of her knife and fork and he glanced up and saw that she was eating rapidly.

"What's the rush?" he murmured. She didn't reply. The noise of her knife and fork went on and then stopped suddenly and he looked up again. He saw she was looking out and away from the table, focusing again on the far end of the counter.

She frowned and resumed eating. He waited a few moments, and then murmured, "I thought you said it ain't your problem."

She let it slide past. She went on frowning. "They're still sitting there. I wish they'd get up and go out."

"I guess they wanna stay here and get warm. It's nice and warm in here."

"It's getting too warm," she said.

"It is?" He sipped more coffee. "I don't feel it."

"Not much you don't." She gave him another sideways look. "Don't give me that cucumber routine. You're sitting on a hot spot and you know it."

"Got a cigarette?"

"I'm talking to you—"

"I heard what you said." He gestured toward her handbag. "Look, I'm all outa smokes. See if you got a spare."

She opened the handbag and took out a pack of cigarettes. She gave him one, took one for herself, and struck a match. As he leaned forward to get the light, she said, "Who are they?"

"You got me."

"Ever see them before?"

"Nope."

"All right," she said. "We'll drop it."

She finished eating, drank some water, took a final puff at her cigarette and put it out in the ashtray. They got up from the booth and walked out of the eatery. Now the wind came harder and colder and it had started to snow. As the flakes hit the pavement they stayed there white instead of melting. She pulled up her coat collar, and put her hands into her pockets. She looked up and around at the snow coming down, and said she liked the snow, she hoped it would keep on snowing. He said it would probably snow all night and then some tomorrow. She asked him if he liked the snow. He said it didn't really matter to him.

They were walking along on the cobblestoned street and

he wanted to look behind him but he didn't. The wind was coming at them and they had to keep their heads down and push themselves along. She was saying he could walk her home if he wanted to. He said all right, not thinking to ask where she lived. She told him she lived in a rooming house on Kenworth Street. She was telling him the block number but he didn't hear. He was listening to the sound of his footsteps and her footsteps and wondering if that was the only sound. Then he heard the other sound, but it was only some alley cats crying. It was a small sound, and he decided they were kittens wailing for their mother. He wished there was something he could do for them, the motherless kittens. They were somewhere in that alley across the street. He heard the waitress saying, "Where you going?"

He had moved away from her, toward the curb. He was looking at the entrance to the alley across the street. She came up to him and said, "What is it?"

"The kittens," he said.

"Kittens?"

"Listen to them," he said. "Poor little kittens. They're having a sad time."

"You got it twisted," she said. "They ain't no kittens, they're grown-up cats. From what I hear, they're having a damn good time."

He listened again, This time he heard it correctly. He grinned and said, "Guess it needs a new aerial."

"No," she said. "The aerial's all right. You just got your stations mixed, that's all."

He didn't quite get that. He looked at her inquiringly.

She said, "I guess it's a habit you got. Like in the Hut. I've noticed it. You never seem to know or care what's really happening. Always tuned in on some weird kinda wave length that only you can hear. As if you ain't concerned in the least with current events."

He laughed softly.

"Quit that," she cut in. "Quit making it a joke. This ain't no joke, what's happening now. You take a look around, you'll see what I mean."

She was facing him, staring past him. He said, "We got company?"

She nodded slowly.

"I don't hear anything," he said, "Only them cats—"

"Forget the cats. You got your hands full now. You can't afford no side shows."

She's got a point there, he thought. He turned and looked down the street. Far down there the yellow-green glow from a street lamp came dripping off the tops of the parked cars. It formed a faintly lit, yellow-green pool on the cobblestones, a shimmering screen for all moving shadows. He saw two shadows moving on the screen, two creepers crouched down there behind one of the parked cars.

"They're waiting," he said. "They're waiting for us to move."

"If we're gonna move, we'd better do it fast." She spoke technically. "Come on, we'll hafta run—"

"No," he said. "There's no rush. We'll just keep walking."

Again she gave him the searching look. "You been through this sorta thing before?"

He didn't answer. He was concentrating on the distance between here and the street corner ahead. They were walking slowly toward the corner. He estimated the distance was some twenty yards. As they went on walking slowly he looked at her and smiled and said, "Don't be nervous. There's nothing to be nervous about."

Not much there ain't, he thought.

They came to the street corner and turned onto a narrow street that had only one lamp. His eyes probed the darkness and found a splintered wooden door, the entrance to an alleyway. He tried the door and it gave, and he went through and she followed him, closing the door behind her. As they stood there, waiting for the sound of approaching footsteps, he heard a rustling noise, as though she was searching for something under her coat.

"What are you doing?" he asked.

"Getting my hatpin," she said. "They come in here, they'll have a five-inch hatpin all ready for them."

"You think it'll bother them?"

"It won't make them happy, that's for sure."

"I guess you're right. That thing goes in deep, it hurts."

"Let them try something." She spoke in a tight whisper, "Just let them try something, and see what happens."

They waited there in the pitch-black darkness behind the alley door. Moments passed, and then they heard the footsteps coming. The footsteps arrived, hesitated, went on and then stopped. Then the footsteps came back toward the alley door. He could feel the rigid stillness of the waitress, close beside him. Then he could hear the voices on the other side of the door.

"Where'd they go?" one of the voices said.

"Maybe into one of these houses."

"We shoulda moved faster."

"We played it right. It's just that they were close to home. They went into one of these houses."

"Well, whaddya want to do?"

"We can't start ringing doorbells."

"You wanta keep walking? Maybe they're somewhere up the street."

"Let's go back to the car. I'm getting cold."

"You wanna call it a night?"

"A loused-up night."

"In spades. God damn it."

The footsteps went away. He said to her, "Let's wait a few minutes," and she said, "I guess I can put the hatpin away."

He grinned and murmured, "Be careful where you put it, I don't wanna get jabbed." They were standing there in the cramped space of the very narrow alley and as her arm moved, her elbow came lightly against his ribs. It wasn't more than a touch, but for some reason he quivered, as though the hatpin had jabbed him. He knew it wasn't the hatpin. And then, moving again, shifting her position in the cramped space, she touched him again and there was more quivering. He breathed in fast through his teeth, feeling something happening. It was happening suddenly and much too fast and he tried to stop it. He said to himself, You gotta stop it. But the thing of it is, it came on you too quick, you just weren't ready for it, you had no idea it was on its way. Well, one thing you know, you can't get rid of it standing here with her so close, too close, too damn close. You think she knows? Sure she knows, she's trying not to touch you again. And now she's moving back so you'll have more room. But it's still too crowded in here. I guess we can go out now. Come on, open the door. What are you waiting for?

He opened the alley door and stepped out onto the pavement. She followed him. They walked up the street, not talking, not looking at each other. He started to walk faster, moving out in front of her. She made no attempt to catch up with him. It went on like that and he was moving far out in front of her, not thinking about it, just wanting to walk fast and get home and go to sleep.

Then presently it occurred to him that he was walking alone. He'd come to a street crossing and he turned and waited. He looked for her and didn't see her. Where'd she go? he asked himself. The answer came from very far down the street, the sound of her clicking heels, going off in the other direction.

For a moment he played with the thought of going after her. So you won't get Z for etiquette, he thought, and took a few steps. Then he stopped, and shook his head, and said to himself, You better leave it the way it is. Stay away from her.

But why? he asked himself, suddenly aware that something was happening again. It just don't figure, it can't be like that, like just the thought of her touching you is a little too much for you to handle and it gets started again. For months she's been working at the Hut, you've seen her there every night and she was nothing more than part of the scenery. And now out of nowhere comes this problem.

You calling it a problem? Come off that, you know it ain't no problem, you just ain't geared for any problems, for any issues at all. With you it's everything for kicks, the cool-easy kicks that ask for no effort at all, the soft-easy style that has you smiling all the time with your tongue in your cheek. It's been that way for a long time now and it's worked for you, it's worked out just fine. You take my advice, you'll keep it that way.

But she said she lived on Kenworth Street. Maybe you better do some scouting, just to make sure she got home all right. Yes, them two operators mighta changed their minds about calling it a night. They coulda decided to have another look around the neighborhood. Maybe they spotted her walking alone and—

Now look, you gotta stop it. You gotta think about something else. Think about what? All right, let's think about Oscar Levant. Is he really talented? Yes, he's really talented. Is Art Tatum talented? Art Tatum is very talented. And what about Walter Geiseking? Well, you never heard him play in person, so you can't say, you just don't know. Another thing you don't know is the house number on Kenworth. You don't even know the block number. Did she tell you the block number? I can't remember.

Oh for Christ's sake go home and go to sleep.

He lived in a rooming house a few blocks away from the Hut. It was a two-story house and his room was on the second floor. The room was small, the rent was five-fifty a week, and it amounted to a bargain because the landlady had a cleanliness phobia; she was always scrubbing or dusting. It was a very old house but all the rooms were spotless.

His room had a bed, a table and a chair. On the floor near the chair there was a pile of magazines. They were all musical publications, most of them dealing with classical music. The magazine on top of the pile was open and as he came into the room he picked it up and leafed through it. Then he started to read an article having to do with some new developments in contrapuntal theory.

The article was very interesting. It was written by a well-known name in the field, someone who really knew what it was all about. He lit a cigarette and stood there under the ceiling light, still wearing his snow-speckled overcoat, focusing on the magazine article. Somewhere in the middle of the third paragraph he lifted his eyes and looked at the window.

The window faced the street; the shade was halfway up. He walked to the window and looked out. Then he opened the window and leaned out to get a wider look. The street was empty. He stayed there and watched the snow coming down. He felt the wind-whipped flakes taking cold bites at his face. The cold air sliced and chopped at him, and he thought, It's gonna feel good to get into that bed.

He undressed quickly. Then he was naked and climbing in under the sheet and the thick quilt, pulling the cord of the lamp near the bed, pulling the other cord that was a long string attached from the ceiling light to the bedpost. He sat there propped against the pillow, and lit another cigarette and continued with the magazine article.

For a few minutes he went on reading, then he just looked at the printed words without taking them in. It went that way for a while, and finally he let the magazine fall to the floor. He sat there smoking and looking at the wall across the room.

The cigarette burned low and he leaned over to smother it in the ashtray on the table near the bed. As he pressed the stub in the tray, he heard the knock on the door.

The wind whistled in through the open window and mixed with the sound that came from the door. He felt very cold, looking at the door, wondering who it was out there.

Then he smiled at himself, knowing who it was, knowing what he'd hear next because he'd heard it so many times in the three years he'd lived here.

From the other side of the door a female voice whispered, "You in there, Eddie? It's me, Clarice."

He climbed out of bed. He opened the door and the woman came in. He said, "Hello, Clarice," and she looked at him standing there naked and said, "Hey, get under that quilt. You'll catch cold."

Then she closed the door, doing it carefully and quietly. He was in the bed again, sitting there with the quilt up around his middle. He smiled at her and said, "Sit down."

She pulled the chair toward the bed and sat down. She said, "Jesus Christ, it's freezing in here," and got up and lowered the window. Then, seated again, she said, "You cold-air fiends amaze me. It's a wonder you don't get the flu. Or ammonia."

"Fresh air is good for you."

"Not this time of year," she said. "This time of year it's for the birds, and even they don't want it. Them birds got more brains than we got. They go to Florida."

"They can do it. They got wings."

"I wish to hell I had wings," the woman said. "Or at least the cash it needs for bus fare. I'd pack up and head south and get me some of that sunshine."

"You ever been south?"

"Sure, loads of times. On the carnival circuit. One time in Jacksonville I busted an ankle, trying out a new caper. They left me stranded there in the hospital, didn't even leave me my pay. Them carnival people—some of them are dogs, just dogs."

She helped herself to one of his cigarettes. She lit it with a loose, graceful motion of arm and wrist. Then she waved out the flaming match, tossing it from one hand to the other, the flame dying in mid-air, and caught the dead match precisely between her thumb and small finger.

"How's that for timing?" she asked him, as though he'd never seen the trick before.

He'd seen it countless times. She was always performing these little stunts. And sometimes at the Hut she'd clear the tables to give herself room, and do the flips and somersaults that showed she still had some of it left, the timing and the coordination and the extra-fast reflexes. In her late teens and early twenties she'd been a better-than-average acrobatic dancer.

Now, at thirty-two, she was still a professional, but in a different line of endeavor. It was all horizontal acrobatics on a mattress, her body for rent at three dollars a performance. In her room down the hall on the second floor she gave them more than their money's worth. Her contortions on the mattress were strictly circus-stunt variety. Among the barflies at the Hut, the consensus was "—really something, that Clarice. You come outa that room, you're dizzy."

Her abilities in this field, especially the fact that she never slackened the pace, were due mainly to her bent for keeping in condition. As a stunt dancer, she'd adhered faithfully to the strict training rules, the rigid diet and the daily exercises. In this present profession, she was equally devoted to certain laws and regulations of physical culture, maintaining that "it's very important, y'unnerstand. Sure, I drink gin. It's good for me. Keeps me from eating too much. I never overload my belly."

Her body showed it. She still had the acrobat's coiled-spring flexibility, and was double-jointed in so many places that it was as if she had no bones at all. She stood five-five and weighed one-five, but she didn't look skinny, just tightly packed around the frame. There wasn't much of breast or hip or thigh, just about enough to label it female. The female aspect showed mainly in her face, her fragile nose and chin, her wide-set, pale-gray eyes. She wore her hair rather short, and was always having it dyed. Right now it was somewhere between yellow and orange.

She sat there wearing a terry cloth bathrobe, one sleeve ripped halfway up to the elbow. With the cigarette still between the thumb and little finger, she lifted it to her mouth, took a small sip of smoke, let it out and said to him, "How's about it?"

"Not tonight."

"You broke?"

He nodded.

Clarice sipped more smoke. She said, "You want it on credit?"

He shook his head.

"You've had it on credit before," she said. "Your credit's always good with me."

"It ain't that," he said. "It's just that I'm tired. I'm awfully tired."

"You wanna go to sleep?" She started to get up.

"No," he said. "Sit there. Stick around a while. We'll talk."

"Okay." She settled back in the chair. "I need some company, anyway. I get so dragged in that room sometimes. They never wanna sit and talk. As if they're afraid I'll charge them extra."

"How'd you do tonight?"

She shrugged. "So-so." She put her hand in the bathrobe pocket and there was the rustling of paper, the tinkling of coins. "For Friday night it wasn't bad, I guess. Most Friday nights there ain't much trade. They either spend their last nickel at Harriet's or they're so plastered they gotta be carried home. Or else they're too noisy and I can't chance it. The lady warned me again last week. She said one more time and out I go."

"She's been saying that for years."

"Sometimes I wonder why she lets me stay."

"You really wanna know?" He smiled dimly. "Her room is right under yours. She could take a different room if she wanted to. After all, it's her house. But no, she keeps that room. So it figures she likes the sound it makes."

"The sound? What sound?"

"The bedsprings," he said.

"But look now, that woman is seventy-six years old."

"That's the point," he said. "They get too old for the action, they gotta have something, at least. With her it's the sound."

Clarice pondered it for a few moments. Then she nodded slowly. "Come to think of it, you got something there." And then, with a sigh, "It must be awful to get old like that."

"You think so? I don't think so. It's just a part of the game and it happens, that's all."

"It won't happen to me," she said decisively. "I hit sixty, I'll take gas. What's the point of hanging around doing nothing?"

"There's plenty to do after sixty."

"Not for this one. This one ain't joining a sewing circle, or playing bingo night after night. If I can't do no better than that, I'll just let them put me in a box."

"They put you in, you'd jump right out. You'd come out doing somersaults."

"You think I would? Really?"

"Sure you would." He grinned at her. "Double somersaults and back flips. And getting applause."

Her face lighted up, as though she could see it happening. But then her bare feet felt the solid floor and it brought her back to here and now. She looked at the man in the bed.

And then she was off the chair and onto the side of the bed. She put her hand on the quilt over his knees.

He frowned slightly. "What's the matter, Clarice?"

"I don't know, I just feel like doing something."

"But I told you—"

"That was business. This ain't business. Reminds me of one night last summer when I came in here and we got to talking, I remember you were flat broke and I said you could have credit and you said no, so I let it drop and we went on talking about this and that and you happened to mention my hair-do. You said it looked real nice, the way I had my hair fixed. I'd fixed it myself earlier that night and I was wondering about how it looked. So of course it gimme a lift when you said that, and I said thanks. I remember saying thanks.

"But I don't know, I guess it needed more than just thanks. I guess I hadda show some real appreciation. Not exactly what you'd call a favor for a favor, but more like an urge, I'd call it. And the windup was I let you have it for free. So now I'll tell you something. I'll tell you the way it went for me. It went all the way up in the sky."

His frown had deepened. And then a grin mixed with the frown and he said, "Watcha doing? Writing verses?"

She gave a little laugh. "Sounds that way, don't it?" And tried it for sound, mimicking herself, "—way up in the sky." She shook her head, and said, "Jesus Christ, I oughtta put that on tape and sell it to the soap people. But even so, what I'm trying to say, that night last summer was some night, Eddie, I sure remember that night."

He nodded slowly. "Me too."

"You remember?" She leaned toward him. "You really remember?"

"Sure," he said. "It was one of them nights don't come very often."

"And here's something else. If I ain't mistaken, it was a Friday night."

"I don't know," he said.

"Sure it was. It damn sure was a Friday night, cause next day at the Hut you got your pay from Harriet. She always pays you on Saturdays and that's how I remember. She paid you and then you came over to the table where I was sitting with some johns. You tried to give me three dollars. I told you to go to hell. So then you wanted to know what I was sore about, and I said I wasn't sore. And just to prove it, I bought you a drink. A double gin."

"That's right," he said, remembering that he hadn't wanted the gin, he'd accepted it just as a gesture. As they'd raised glasses, she'd been looking through her glass and through his glass, as though trying to tell him something that could only be said through the gin. He remembered that now. He remembered it very clearly.

He said, "I'm really tired, Clarice. If I wasn't—"

Her hand went away from the quilt over his knee. She gave a little shrug and said, "Well, I guess all Friday nights ain't the same."

He winced slightly.

She walked toward the door. At the door she turned and gave him a friendly smile. He started to say something, but he couldn't get it out. He saw that her smile had given way to a look of concern.

"What is it, Eddie?"

He wondered what showed on his face. He was trying to show the soft-easy smile, but he couldn't get it started. Then he blinked several times and made a straining effort and the smile came onto his lips.

But she was looking at his eyes. "You sure you're all right?"

"I'm fine," he said. "Why shouldn't I be? I got no worries."

She winked at him, as though to say, You want me to believe that, I'll believe it. Then she said good night and walked out of the room.

He didn't get much sleep. He thought about Turley. He said to himself, Why think about that? You know they didn't get Turley. If they'd grabbed Turley, they wouldn't need you. They came after you because they're very anxious to have some discussion with Turley. What about? Well, you don't know, and you don't care. So I guess you can go to sleep now.

He thought about the beer cases falling onto the floor at the Hut. When you did that, he thought, you started something. Like telling them you had some connection with Turley. And naturally they snatched at that. They reasoned you could take them to Turley.

But I guess it's all right now. Item one, they don't know you're his brother. Item two, they don't know where you live. We'll skip item three because that item is the waitress and you don't want to think about her. All right, we won't think about her, we'll concentrate on Turley. You know he got away and that's nice to know. It's also nice to know they won't get you. After all, they're not the law, they can't go around asking questions. Not in this neighborhood anyway. In this neighborhood it sure as hell ain't easy to get information. The citizens here have a closed-mouth policy when it comes to giving out facts and figures, especially someone's address. You've lived here long enough to know that. You know there's a very stiff line of defense against all bill collectors, skip tracers, or any kind of tracers. So no matter who they ask, they'll get nothing. But hold it there. You sure about that?

I'm sure of only one thing, mister. You need sleep and you can't sleep. You've started something and you're making it big, and the truth is it ain't nothing at all. That's just about the size of it, it's way down there at zero.

His eyes were open and he was looking at the window. In the darkness he could see the white dots moving on the black screen, the millions of white dots coming down out there, and he thought, They're gonna have sledding today, the kids. Say, is that window open? Sure it's open, you can see it's open. You opened it after Clarice walked out. Well, let's open it wider. We have more air in here, it might help us to fall asleep.

He got out of bed and went to the window. He opened it all the way. Then he leaned out and looked and the street was empty. In bed again, he closed his eyes and kept them closed and finally fell asleep. He slept for less than an hour and got up and went to the window and looked out. The street was empty. Then he had another couple hours of sleep before he felt the need for one more look. At the window, leaning out, he looked at the street and saw that it was empty. That's final, he told himself. We won't look again.

It was six-fifteen, the numbers yellow-white on the face of the alarm clock. We'll get some sleep now, some real sleep, he decided. We'll sleep till one, or make it one-thirty. He set the clock for one-thirty and climbed into bed and fell asleep. At eight he woke up and went to the window. Then he returned to the bed and slept until ten-twenty, at which time he made another trip to the window. The only action out there was the snow. It came down in thick flurries, and already it looked a few inches deep. He watched it for some moments, then climbed into bed and fell asleep. Two hours later he was up and at the window. There was nothing happening and he went back to sleep. Within thirty minutes he was awake and at the window. The street was empty, except for the Buick.

The Buick was brand-new, a pale green-and-cream hard-top convertible. It was parked across the street and from the angle of the window he could see them in the front seat, the two of them. He recognized the felt hats first, the pearl-gray and the darker gray. It's them, he told himself. And you knew they'd show. You've known it all night long. But how'd they get the address?

Let's find out. Let's get dressed and go out there and find out.

Getting dressed, he didn't hurry. They'll wait, he thought. They're in no rush and they don't mind waiting. But it's cold out there, you shouldn't make them wait too long, it's inconsiderate. After all, they were thoughtful of you, they were really considerate. They didn't come up here and break down the door and drag you out of bed. I think that was very nice of them.

He slipped into the tattered overcoat, went out of the room, down the steps, and out the front door. He walked across the snow-covered street and they saw him coming. He was smiling at them. As he came closer, he gave a little wave of recognition, and the man behind the wheel waved back. It was the short, thin one, the one in the pearl-gray hat.

The car window came down, and the man behind the wheel said, "Hello, Eddie."

"Eddie?"

"That's your name, ain't it?"

"Yes, that's my name." He went on smiling. His eyes were taking the mild inquiry, Who told you?

Without sound the short, thin one answered, Let's skip that for now, then said aloud, "They call me Feather. It's sort of a nickname. I'm in that weight division." He indicated the other man, saying, "This is Morris."

"Pleased to meet you," Eddie said.

"Same here," Feather said. "We're very pleased to meet you, Eddie." Then he reached back and opened the rear door. "Why stand out there in the snow? Slide in and get comfortable."

"I'm comfortable," Eddie said.

Feather held the door open. "It's warmer in the car."

"I know it is," Eddie said. "I'd rather stay out here. I like it out here."

Feather and Morris looked at each other. Morris moved his hand toward his lapel, his fingers sliding under and in, and Feather said, "Leave it alone. We don't need that."

"I wanna show it to him," Morris said.

"He knows it's there."

"Maybe he ain't sure. I want him to be sure."

"All right, show it to him."

Morris reached in under his lapel and took out a small black revolver. It was chunky and looked heavy but he handled it as though it were a fountain pen. He twirled it once and it came down flat in his palm. He let it stay there for a few moments, then returned it to the holster under his lapel. Feather was saying to Eddie, "You wanna get in the car?"

"No," Eddie said.

Again Feather and Morris looked at each other. Morris said, "Maybe he thinks we're kidding."

"He knows we're not kidding."

Morris said to Eddie, "Get in the car. You gonna get in the car?"

"If I feel like it." Eddie was smiling again. "Right now I don't feel like it."

Morris frowned. "What's the matter with you? You can't be that stupid. Maybe you're sick in the head, or something." And then, to Feather, "How's he look to you?"

Feather was studying Eddie's face. "I don't know," he murmured slowly and thoughtfully. "He looks like he can't feel anything."

"He can feel metal," Morris said. "He gets a chunk of metal in his face, he'll feel it."

Eddie stood there next to the opened window, his hands going through his pocket and hunting for cigarettes. Feather asked him what he was looking for and he said, "A smoke," but there were no cigarettes and finally Feather gave him one and lit it for him and then said, "I'll give you more if you want. I'll give you an entire pack. If that ain't enough, I'll give you a carton. Or maybe you'd rather have cash."

Eddie didn't say anything.

"How's fifty dollars?" Morris said, smiling genially at Eddie.

"What would that buy me?" He wasn't looking at either of them.

"A new overcoat," Morris said. "You could use a new overcoat."

"I think he wants more than that," Feather said, again studying Eddie's face. He was waiting for Eddie to say something. He waited for some fifteen seconds, then said, "You want to quote a figure?"

Eddie spoke very softly. "For what? What am I selling?"

"You know," Feather said. And then, "A hundred?"

Eddie didn't reply. He was grazing slantwise through the opened window, through the windshield, and past the hood of the Buick.

"Three hundred?" Feather asked.

"That covers a lot of expenses," Morris put in.

"I ain't got much expenses," Eddie said.

"Then why you stalling?" Feather asked mildly.

"I'm not stalling," Eddie said. "I'm just thinking."

"Maybe he thinks we ain't got that kind of money," Morris said.

"Is that what's holding up the deal?" Feather said to Eddie. "You wanna see the roll?"

Eddie shrugged.

"Sure, let him see it," Morris said. "Let him know we're not just talking, we got the solid capital."

Feather reached into the inner pocket of his jacket and took out a shiny lizard billfold. His fingers went in and came out with a sheaf of crisp currency. He counted it aloud, as though counting it for himself, but loud enough for Eddie to hear. There were twenties and fifties and hundreds. The total was well over two thousand dollars. Feather returned the money to the billfold and put it back in his pocket.

"That's a lot of money to carry around," Eddie commented.

"That's chicken feed," Feather said.

"Depends on the annual income," Eddie murmured. "You make a bundle, you can carry a bundle. Or sometimes it ain't yours, they just give it to you to spend."

"They?" Feather narrowed his eyes. "Who you mean by they?"

Eddie shrugged again. "I mean, when you work for big people—"

Feather glanced at Morris. For some moments it was quiet. Then Feather said to Eddie, "You wouldn't be getting cute, would you?"

Eddie smiled at the short, thin man and made no answer.

"Do yourself a favor," Feather said quietly. "Don't be cute with me. I'll only get irritated and then we can't talk business. I'll be too upset." He was looking at the steering wheel. He played his thin fingers around the smooth rim of the steering wheel. "Now let's see. Where were we?"

"It was three," Morris offered. "He wouldn't sell at three. So what I think is, you offer him five—"

"All right," Feather said. He looked at Eddie. "Five hundred dollars."

Eddie glanced down at the cigarette between his fingers. He lifted it to his mouth and took a meditative drag.

"Five hundred," Feather said. "And no more."

"That's final?"

"Capped," Feather said, and reached inside his jacket, going for the billfold.

"Nothing doing," Eddie said.

Feather exchanged another look with Morris. "I don't get this," Feather said. He spoke as though Eddie weren't there. "I've seen all kinds, but this one here is new to me. What gives with him?"

"You're asking me?" Morris made a hopeless gesture, his palms out and up. "I can't reach out that far. He's moon material."

Eddie was wearing the soft-easy smile and gazing at nothing. He stood there taking small drags at the cigarette. His overcoat was unbuttoned, as though he weren't aware of wind and snow. The two men in the car were staring at him, waiting for him to say something, to give some indication that he was actually there.

And finally, from Feather, "All right, let's try it from another angle." His voice was mild. "It's this way, Eddie. All we wanna do is talk to him. We're not out to hurt him."

"Hurt who?"

Feather snapped his fingers. "Come on, let's put it on the table. You know who I'm talking about. Your brother. Your brother Turley."

Eddie's expression didn't change. He didn't even blink. He was saying to himself, Well, there it is. They know you're his brother. So now you're in it, you're pulled in and I wish you could figure a way to slide out.

He heard Feather saying, "We just wanna sit him down and have a little talk. All you gotta do is make the connection."

"I can't do that," he said. "I don't know where he is."

Then, from Morris, "You sure about that? You sure you ain't trying to protect him?"

"Why should I?" Eddie shrugged. "He's only my brother. For half a grand I'd be a fool not to hand him over. After all, what's a brother? A brother means nothing."

"Now he's getting cute again," Feather said.

"A brother, a mother, a father," Eddie said with another shrug, "they ain't important at all. Like merchandise you sell across a counter. That is," and his voice dropped just a little, "according to certain ways of thinking."

"What's he saying now?" Morris wanted to know.

"I think he's telling us to go to hell," Feather said. Then he looked at Morris, and he nodded slowly, and Morris took out the revolver. Then Feather said to Eddie, "Open the door. Get in."

Eddie stood there smiling at them.

"He wants it," Morris said, and then there was the sound of the safety catch.

"That's a pretty noise," Eddie said.

"You wanna hear something really pretty?" Feather murmured.

"First you gotta count to five," Eddie told him. "Go on, count to five, I wanna hear you count."

Feather's thin face was powder-white. "Let's make it three." But as he said it he was looking past Eddie.

Eddie was saying, "All right, we'll count to three. You want me to count for you?"

"Later," Feather said, still looking past him, and smiling now. "That is, when she gets here."

Just then Eddie felt the snow and the wind. The wind was very cold. He heard himself saying, "When who gets here?"

"The skirt," Feather said. "The skirt we saw you with last night. She's coming to pay you a visit."

He turned and saw her coming down the street. She was crossing the street diagonally, coming toward the car. He raised his hand just high enough to make the warning gesture, telling her to stay away, to please stay away. She kept advancing toward the car and he thought, She knows, she knows you're in a situation and she figures she can help. But that gun. She can't see that gun—

He heard the voice of Feather saying, "She your girl friend, Eddie?"

He didn't answer. The waitress came closer. He made another warning gesture but now she was very close and he looked away from her to glance inside the car. He saw Morris sitting slantwise with the gun moving slowly from side to side, to cover two people instead of one. That does it, he thought. That includes her in.

Then she was standing there next to him and they were both looking at the gun. He waited for her to ask him what it was all about, but she didn't say anything. Feather leaned back, smiling at them, giving them plenty of time to study the gun, to think about the gun. It went on that way for perhaps half a minute, and then Feather said to Eddie, "That counting routine. You still want me to count to three?"

"No," Eddie said. "I guess that ain't necessary." He was trying not to frown. He was very much annoyed with the waitress.

"What's the seating arrangement?" Morris wanted to know.

"You in the back," Feather told him, then took the gun from Morris and opened the door and got out of the car. He held the gun close to his side as he walked with Eddie and Lena, staying just a little behind them as they went around to the other side of the car. He told them to get in the front seat. Eddie started to get in first, and Feather said, "No, I want her in the middle." She climbed in and Eddie followed her. Morris was reaching out from the back seat to take the gun from Feather. For just an instant there was a chance for interception, but it wasn't much of a chance and Eddie thought, No matter how quick you are, the gun is quicker. You go for it, it'll go for you. And you know it'll get there first. I guess we'd better face the fact that we're going on a trip somewheres.

He watched Feather climbing in behind the wheel. The waitress sat there looking straight ahead through the windshield. "Sit back," Feather said to her. "You might as well be comfortable." Without looking at Feather, she said, "Thanks," and leaned back, folding her arms. Then Feather started the engine.

The Buick cruised smoothly down the street, turned a corner, went down another narrow street and then moved onto a wider street. Feather switched on the radio. A cool jazz outfit was in the middle of something breezy. It was nicely modulated music, featuring a soft-toned saxophone and someone's light expert touch on the keyboard. That's very fine piano, Eddie said to himself. I think that's Bud Powell.

Then he heard Lena saying, "Where we going?"

"Ask your boy friend," Feather said.

"He's not my boy friend."

"Well, ask him anyway. He's the navigator."

She looked at Eddie. He shrugged and went on listening to the music.

"Come on," Feather said to him. "Start navigating."

"Where you wanna go?"

"Turley."

"Where's that?" Lena asked.

"It ain't a town," Feather said. "It's his brother. We got some business with his brother."

"The man from last night?" She put the question to
Eddie. "The one who ran out of the Hut?"

He nodded. "They did some checking," he said. "First
they find out he's my brother. Then they get more information. They get my address."

"Who told them?"

"I think I know," he said. "But I'm not sure."

"I'll straighten you," Feather offered. "We went back to
that saloon when it opened up this morning. We buy a few
drinks and then we get to talking with big-belly, I mean the
one who looks like a has-been wrestler—"

"Plyne," the waitress said.

"Is that his name?" Feather hit the horn lightly and two
very young sledders jumped back on the curb. "So we're
there at the bar and he's getting friendly, he's telling us he's
the general manager and he gives us a drink on the house.
Then he talks about this and that, staying clear of the point
he wants to make. He handles it all right for a while, but
finally it's too much for him, and he's getting clumsy with
the talk. We just stand there and look at him. Then he
makes his pitch. He wants to know what our game is."

"He said it kind of hungry-like," from Morris in the back
seat.

"Yeah," Feather said. "Like he has it tabbed we're big
time and he's looking for an in. You know how it is with
these has-beens, they all want to get right up there again."

"Not all of them," the waitress said. And just for a
moment she glanced at Eddie. And then, turning again to
Feather, "You were saying?"

"Well, we didn't give him anything, just some nowhere
talk that only made him hungrier. And then, just tossing it
away, as if it ain't too important, I mention our friend here
who knocked down them beer cases. It was a long shot,
sure. But it paid off." He smiled congenially at Eddie. "It
paid off real nice."

"That Plyne," the waitress said. "That Plyne and his big
mouth."

"He got paid off, too," Feather said. "I slipped him a
half-C for the info."

"That fifty made his eyes pop," Morris said.

"And made him greedy for more." Feather laughed

lightly. "He asked us to come around again. He said if there was anything more he could do, we should call on him and—"

"The pig," she said. "The filthy pig."

Feather went on laughing. He looked over his shoulder, saying to Morris, "Come to think of it, that's what he looked like. I mean, when he went for the fifty. Like a pig going for slop—"

Morris pointed toward the windshield. "Watch where you're going."

Feather stopped laughing. "Who's got the wheel?"

"You got the wheel," Morris said. "But look at all the snow, it's freezing. We don't have chains."

"We don't need chains," Feather said. "We got snow tires."

"Well, even so," Morris said, "you better drive careful."

Again Feather looked at him. "You telling me how to drive?"

"For Christ's sake," Morris said. "I'm only telling you—"

"Don't tell me how to drive. I don't like when they tell me how to drive."

"When it snows, there's always accidents," Morris said. "We wanna get where we're going—"

"That's a sensible statement," Feather said. "Except for one thing. We don't know where we're going yet."

Then he glanced inquiringly at Eddie.

Eddie was listening to the music from the radio.

Feather reached toward the instrument panel and switched off the radio. He said to Eddie, "We'd like to know where we're going. You wanna help us out on that a little?"

Eddie shrugged. "I told you, I don't know where he is."

"You haven't any idea? No idea at all?"

"It's a big city," Eddie said. "It's a very big city."

"Maybe he ain't in the city," Feather murmured.

Eddie blinked a few times. He was looking straight ahead. He sensed that the waitress was watching him.

Feather probed gently. "I said maybe he ain't in the city. Maybe he's in the country."

"What?" Eddie said. All right, he told himself. Easy, now. Maybe he's guessing.

"The country," Feather said. "Like, say, in New Jersey."

That does it, Eddie thought. That wasn't a guess.

"Or let's tighten it a little," Feather said. "Let's make it South Jersey."

Now Eddie looked at Feather. He didn't say anything. The waitress sat there between them, quiet and relaxed, her hands folded in her lap.

Morris said, sort of mockingly, with pretended ignorance, "What's this with South Jersey? What's in South Jersey?"

"Watermelons," Feather said. "That's where they grow them."

"The melons?" Morris was playing straight man. "Who grows them?"

"The farmers, stupid. There's a lotta farmers in South Jersey. There's all these little farms, these watermelon patches."

"Where?"

"Whaddya mean, where? I just told you where. In South Jersey."

"The watermelon trees?"

"Pipe that," Feather said to the two front-seat passengers. "He thinks they grow on trees." And then, to Morris, "They grow in the ground. Like lettuce."

"Well, I've seen them growing lettuce, but never watermelons. How come I ain't seen the watermelons?"

"You didn't look."

"Sure I looked. I always look at the scenery. Especially in South Jersey. I've been to South Jersey loads of times. To Cape May. To Wildwood. All down through there."

"No watermelons?"

"Not a one," Morris said.

"I guess you were driving at night," Feather told him.

"Could be," Morris said. And then, timing it, "Or maybe these farms are far off the road."

"Now, that's an angle." Feather took a quick look at Eddie, then purred, "Some of these farms are way back there in the woods. These watermelon patches, I mean. They're sorta hidden back there—"

"All right, all right," the waitress broke in. She turned to Eddie. "What are they talking about?"

"It's nothing," Eddie said.

"You wish it was nothing," Morris said.

She turned to Feather. "What is it?"

"His folks," Feather said. Again he looked at Eddie. "Go on, tell her. You might as well tell her."

"Tell her what?" Eddie spoke softly. "What's there to tell?"

"There's plenty," Morris said. "That is, if you're in on it." He moved the gun forward just a little, doing it gently, so that the barrel barely touched Eddie's shoulder. "You in on it?"

"Hey, for Christ's sake—" Eddie pulled his shoulder away.

"What's happening there?" Feather asked.

"He's afraid of the rod," Morris said.

"Sure he's afraid. So am I. Put that thing away. We hit a bump it might go off."

"I want him to know—"

"He knows. They both know. They don't have to feel it to know it's there."

"All right." Morris sounded grumpy. "All right, all right."

The waitress was looking at Feather, then at Eddie, then at Feather again. She said, "Well, if he can't tell me, maybe you can—"

"About his folks?" Feather smiled. "Sure, I got some facts. There's the mother and the father and the two brothers. There's this Turley and the other one, his name is Clifton. That right, Eddie?"

Eddie shrugged. "If you say so."

"You know what I think?" Morris said slowly. "I think he's in on it."

"In on what?" the waitress snapped. "At least you could give me some idea—"

"You'll get the idea," Feather told her. "You'll get it when we reach that house."

"What house?"

"In South Jersey," Feather said. "In them woods where it used to be a watermelon patch but the weeds closed in and now it ain't a farm any more. It's just an old wooden house with a lot of weeds around it. And then the woods. There's no other houses around for miles—"

"No roads, either," Morris put in.

"Not cement roads, anyway," Feather said. "Just wagon paths that take you deep in them woods. So all you see is trees and more trees. And finally, there it is, the house. Just that one house far away from everything. It's what I'd call a gloomy layout." He looked at Eddie. "We got no time for fooling around. You know the route, so what you do is, you give the directions."

"How come?" the waitress asked. "Why do you need directions? You pictured that house like you've been there."

"I've never been there," Feather said. He went on looking at Eddie. "I was told about it, that's all. But they left out something. Forgot to tell me how to get there."

"He'll tell you," Morris said.

"Sure he'll tell me. What else can he do?"

Morris nudged Eddie's shoulder. "Give."

"Not yet," Feather said. "Wait'll we cross the bridge into Jersey. Then he'll tell us what roads to take."

"Maybe he don't know," the waitress said.

"You kidding?" Feather flipped it at her. "He was born and raised in that house. For him it's just a trip to the country, to visit the folks."

"Like coming home for Thanksgiving," Morris said. Again he touched Eddie's shoulder. This time it was a friendly pat. "After all, there's no place like home."

"Except it ain't a home," Feather said softly. "It's a hide-out."

Now they were on Front Street, headed south toward the Delaware River Bridge. They were coming into heavy traffic, and south of Lehigh Avenue the street was jammed. In addition to cars and trucks, there was a slow-moving swarm of Saturday afternoon shoppers, some of them jaywalkers who kept their heads down against the wind and the snow. The Buick moved very slowly and Feather kept hitting the horn. Morris was cursing the pedestrians. In front of the Buick there was a very old car without chains. It also lacked a windshield wiper. It was traveling at approximately fifteen miles per hour.

"Give him the horn," Morris said. "Give him the horn again."

"He can't hear it," Feather said.

"Give him the goddam horn. Keep blowing it."

Feather pressed the chromed rim, and the horn blasted and kept blasting. In the car ahead the driver turned and scowled and Feather went on blowing the horn.

"Try to pass him," Morris said.

"I can't," Feather muttered. "The street ain't wide enough."

"Try it now. There's no cars coming now."

Feather steered the Buick toward the left and then out a little more. He started to cut past the old car and then a bread truck came riding in for what looked to be a head-on collision.

Feather pulled hard at the wheel and got back just in time.

"You shoulda kept on," Morris said. "You had enough room."

Feather didn't say anything.

A group of middle-aged women crossed the street between the Buick and the car in front of it. They seemed utterly oblivious to the existence of the Buick. Feather slammed his foot against the brake pedal.

"What're you stopping for?" Morris yelled. "They wanna get hit, then hit them!"

"That's right," the waitress said. "Smash into them. Grind them to a pulp."

The women passed and the Buick started forward. Then a flock of children darted through and the Buick was stopped again.

Morris opened the window at his side and leaned out and shouted, "What the hell's wrong with you?"

"Drop dead," one of the children said. It was a girl about seven years old.

"I'll break your little neck for you," Morris shouted at her.

"That's all right," the child sang back. "Just stay off my blue suede shoes."

The other children began singing the rock-and-roll tune,

"Blue Suede Shoes," twanging on imaginary guitars and imitating various dynamic performers. Morris closed the window, gritting, "Goddam juvenile delinquents."

"Yes, it's quite a problem," the waitress said.

"You shut up," Morris told her.

She turned to Eddie. "The trouble is, there ain't enough playgrounds. We oughtta have more playgrounds. That would get them off the street."

"Yes," Eddie said. "The people ought to do something. It's a very serious problem."

She turned her head and looked back at Morris. "What do you think about it? You got an opinion?"

Morris wasn't listening. He had the window open again and he was leaning out, concentrating on the oncoming traffic. He called to Feather, "It's clear now. Go ahead—"

Feather started to turn the wheel. Then he changed his mind and pulled back in behind the car in front. A moment later a taxicab came whizzing from the other direction. It made a yellow blur as it sped past.

"You coulda made it," Morris complained. "You had plenty of time—"

Feather didn't say anything.

"You gotta cut through while you got the chance," Morris said. "Now if I had that wheel—"

"You want the wheel?" Feather asked.

"All I said was—"

"I'll give you the wheel," Feather said. "I'll wrap it around your neck."

"Don't get excited," Morris said.

"Just leave me alone and let me drive. Is that all right?"

"Sure." Morris shrugged. "You're the driver. You know how to drive."

"Then keep quiet." Feather faced the windshield again. "If there's one thing I can do, it's handle a car. There ain't nobody can tell me about that. I can make a car do anything—"

"Except get through traffic," Morris remarked.

Again Feather's head turned. His eyes were dull-cold, aiming at the tall, thin man. "What are you doing? You trying to irritate me?"

"No," Morris said. "I'm only making talk."

Feather went on looking at him. "I don't need that talk. You give that talk to someone else. You tell someone else how to drive."

Morris pointed to the windshield. "Keep your eyes on the traffic—"

"You just won't let up, will you?" Feather shifted slightly in his seat, to get a fuller look at the man in the rear of the car. "Now I'm gonna tell you something, Morris. I'm gonna tell you—"

"Watch the light," Morris shouted, and gestured wildly toward the windshield. "You got a red light—"

Feather kept looking at him. "I'm telling you, Morris. I'm telling you for the last time—"

"The light," Morris screeched. "It's red, it's red, it says stop—"

The Buick was some twenty feet from the intersection when Feather took his foot off the gas pedal, then lightly stepped on the brake. The car was coming to a stop and Eddie glanced at the waitress, saw that she was focusing slantwise to the other side of the intersecting street, where a black-and-white Police car was double-parked, the two policemen standing out there talking to the driver of a truck parked in a no-parking zone. Eddie had seen the police car and he'd wondered if the waitress would see it and would know what to do about it. He thought, This is the time for it, there won't be another time.

The waitress moved her left leg and her foot came down full force on the accelerator. Pedestrians leaped out of the way as the Buick went shooting past the red light and narrowly missed a westbound car, then stayed southbound going across the trolley tracks and lurching now as Feather hit the brake while the waitress kept her foot on the accelerator. An east-bound trailer made a frantic turn and went up on the pavement. Some women screamed, there was considerably activity on the pavement, brakes screeched, and, finally, a policeman's whistle shrilled through the air.

The Buick was stopped on the south side of the trolley tracks. Feather sat there leaning back, looking sideways at the waitress. Eddie was watching the policeman, who was yelling at the driver of the trailer, telling him to back off the pavement. There was no one hurt, although several of the pedestrians were considerably unnerved. A few women were yelling incoherently, pointing accusingly at the Buick. Then, gradually, a crowd closed in on the Buick. In the Buick there was no talk at all. Around the car the crowd thickened. Feather was still looking at the waitress. Eddie glanced into the rear-view mirror and saw Morris with his hat off. Morris had the hat in his hands and was gazing stupidly at the crowd outside the window. Some of the people in the crowd were saying things to Feather. Then the crowd moved to make a path for the policeman from the black-and-white car. Eddie saw that the other policeman was still occupied with the parking violator. He turned his head slowly and the waitress was looking at him. It seemed she was waiting for him to say something or do something. Her eyes said to him, It's your play, from here on in it's up to you. He made a very slight gesture, pointing to himself, as if saying, All right, I'll handle it. I'll do the talking.

The policeman spoke quietly to Feather. "Let's clear this traffic. Get her over there to the curb." The Buick moved slowly across the remainder of the intersection, the policeman walking along with it, guiding the driver to the southeast corner. "Cut the engine," the policeman told Feather. "Get out of the car."

Feather switched off the engine and opened the door and got out. The crowd went on making noise. A man said, "He's stewed. He's gotta be stewed to drive like that." And an elderly woman shouted, "We just ain't safe any more. We venture out we take our lives in our hands—"

The policeman moved in close to Feather and said, "How many?" and Feather answered, "All I had was two officer. I'll drive you back to the bar, and you can ask the bartender." The policeman looked Feather up and down. "All right, so you're not drunk. Then how do you account for this?" As Feather opened his mouth to reply, Eddie cut in quickly, saying, "He just can't drive, that's all. He's a lousy driver." Feather turned and looked at Eddie. And Eddie went on, "He always gets rattled in traffic." Then he turned to the waitress, saying, "Come on, honey. We don't need this. We'll take a trolley."

"Can't hardly blame you," the policeman said to them as they got out of the car. From the back seat, Morris called out,

"See you later, Eddie," and for a moment there was indecision. Eddie glanced toward the policeman, thinking, You wanna tell the cop what's happening? You figure it's better that way? No, he decided. It's probably better this way.

"Later," Morris called to them as they moved off through the crowd. The waitress stopped and looked back at Morris. "Yeah, give us a call," and she waved at the tall, thin man in the Buick, "we'll be waiting—"

They went on moving through the crowd. Then they were walking north on Front Street. The snow had slackened somewhat. It was slightly warmer now, and the sun was trying to come out. But the wind had not lessened, there was still a bite in it, and Eddie thought, There's gonna be more snow, that sky looks strictly from changeable weather. It could be a blizzard coming.

He heard the waitress saying, "Let's get off this street."

"They won't circle back."

"They might."

"I don't think they will," he said. "When that cop gets finished with them, they're gonna be awfully tired. I think they'll go to a movie or a Turkish bath or something. They've had enough for one day."

"He said he'd see us later."

"You gave him a good answer. You said we'd be waiting. That gives them something to think about. They'll really think about that."

"For how long?" She looked at him. "How long until they try again?"

He made an offhand gesture. "Who knows? Why worry?"

She mimicked his gesture, his indifferent tone. "Well, maybe you're right. Except for one little angle. That thing he had wasn't a water pistol. If they come looking for us, it might be something to worry about."

He didn't say anything. They were walking just a little faster now. "Well?" she said, and he didn't answer. She said it again. She was watching his face and waiting for an answer. "How about it?" she asked, and took hold of his arm. They came to a stop and stood facing each other.

"Now look," he said, and smiled dimly. "This ain't your problem."

She shifted her weight onto one leg, put her hand on her hip and said, "I didn't quite get that."

"It's simple enough. I'm only repeating what you said last night, I thought you meant it. Anyway, I was hoping you meant it."

"In other words," and she took a deep breath, "you're telling me to mind my own damn business."

"Well, I wouldn't put it that way—"

"Why not?" She spoke a trifle louder. "Don't be so polite."

He gazed past her, his smile very soft. "Let's not get upset—"

"You're too goddam polite," she said. "You wanna make a point, make it. Don't walk all around it."

His smile fell away. He tried to build it again. It wouldn't build. Don't look at her, he told himself. You look at her, it'll start like it started last night in that alley when she was standing close to you.

She's close now, come to think of it. She's much too close. He took a backward step, went on gazing past her, then heard himself saying, "I don't need this."

"Need what?"

"Nothing," he mumbled. "Let it ride."

"It's riding."

He winced. He took a step toward her. What are you doing? he asked himself. Then he was shaking his head, trying to clear his brain. It was no go. He felt very dizzy.

He heard her saying, "Well, I might as well know who I'm riding with."

"We're not riding now," he said, and tried to make himself believe it. He grinned at her. "We're just standing here and gabbing."

"Is that what it is?"

"Sure," he said. "That's all it is. What else could it be?"

"I wouldn't know." Her face was expressionless. "That is, I wouldn't know unless I was told."

I'll let that pass, he said to himself. I'd better let it pass. But look at her, she's waiting. But it's more than that, she's aching. She's aching for you to say something.

"Let's walk," he said. "It's no use standing here."

"You're right," she said with a little smile. "It sure ain't getting us anywhere. Come on, let's walk."

They resumed walking north on Front Street. Now they were walking slowly and there was no talk. They went on for several blocks without speaking and then she stopped again and said to him, "I'm sorry, Eddie."

"Sorry? About what?"

"Butting in. I shoulda kept my long nose out of it."

"It ain't a long nose. It's just about right."

"Thanks," she said. They were standing outside a five-and-dime. She glanced toward the display window. "I think I'll do some shopping—"

"I'd better go in with you."

"No," she said. "I can make it alone."

"Well, what I mean is, just in case they—"

"Look, you said there was nothing to worry about. You got them going to the movies or a Turkish bath—"

"Or Woolworth's," he cut in. "They might walk into this Woolworth's."

"What if they do?" She gave a little shrug. "It ain't me they want, it's you."

"That cuts it nice." He smiled at her. "Except it don't cut that way at all. They got you tabbed now. Tied up with me. Like as if we're a team—"

"A team?" She looked away from him. "Some team. You won't even tell me the score."

"On what?"

"South Jersey. That house in the woods. Your family—"

"The score on that is zero," he said. "I got no idea what's happening there."

"Not even a hint?" She gave him a side glance.

He didn't reply. He thought, What can you tell her? What the hell can you tell her when you just don't know?

"Well," she said, "whatever it is, you sure kept it away from that cop. I mean the way you played it, not telling the cop about the gun. To keep the law out of this. Or, let's say, to keep your family away from the law. Something along that line?"

"Yes," he said. "It's along that line."

"Anything more?"

"Nothing," he said. "I know from nothing."

"All right," she said. "All right, Edward."

There was a rush of quiet. It was like a valve opening and the quiet rushing in.

"Or is it Eddie?" she asked herself aloud. "Well, now it's Eddie. It's Eddie at the old piano, at the Hut. But years ago it was Edward—"

He waved his hand sideways, begging her to stop it.

She said, "It was Edward Webster Lynn, the concert pianist, performing at Carnegie Hall."

She turned away and walked into the five-and-dime.

So there it is, he said to himself. But how did she know? What tipped her off? I think we ought to examine that. Or maybe it don't need examining. It stands to reason she remembered something. It must have hit her all at once. That's it, that's the way it usually happens. It came all at once, the name and the face and the music. Or the music and the name and the face. All mixed in there together from seven years ago.

When did it hit her? She's been working at the Hut for four months, six nights a week. Until last night she hardly knew you were alive. So let's have a look at that. Did something happen last night? Did you pull some fancy caper on that keyboard? Just a bar or two of Bach, maybe? Or Brahms or Schumann or Chopin? No. You know who told her. It was Turley.

Sure as hell it was Turley when he went into that booby-hatch raving, when he jumped up and gave that lecture on musical appreciation and the currently sad state of culture in America, claiming that you didn't belong in the Hut, it was the wrong place, the wrong piano, the wrong audience. He screamed it oughtta be a concert hall, with the gleaming grand piano, the diamonds gleaming on the white throats, the full-dress shirt fronts in the seven-fifty orchestra seats. That was what hit her.

But hold it there for just a minute. What's the hookup there? How does she come to Carnegie Hall? She ain't from the classical groove, the way she talks she's from the honkytonk school. Or no, you don't really know what school she's from. The way a person talks has little or nothing to do with the schooling. You ought to know that. Just listen to the way you talk.

What I mean is, the way Eddie talks. Eddie spills words like "ain't" and says "them there" and "this here" and so forth. You know Edward never talked that way. Edward was educated, and an artist, and had a cultured manner of speaking. I guess it all depends where you're at and what you're doing and the people you hang around with. The Hut is a long way off from Carnegie Hall. *Yes.* And it's a definite fact that Eddie has no connection with Edward. You cut all them wires a long time ago. It was a clean split.

Then why are you drifting back? Why pick it up again? Well, just to look at it. Won't hurt to have a look. Won't hurt? You kidding? You can feel the hurt already, as though it's happening again. The way it happened.

It was deep in the woods of South Jersey, in the wooden house that overlooked the watermelon patch. His early childhood was mostly on the passive side. As the youngest of three brothers he was more or less a small, puzzled spectator, unable to understand Clifton's knavery or Turley's rowdyism. They were always at it, and when they weren't pulling capers in the house they were out roaming the countryside. Their special meat was chickens. They were experts at stealing chickens. Or sometimes they'd try for a shoat. They were seldom caught. They'd slide out of trouble or fight their way out of it and, on a few occasions, in their middle teens, they shot their way out of it.

The mother called them bad boys, then shrugged and let it go at that. The mother was an habitual shrugger who'd run out of gas in her early twenties, surrendering to farmhouse drudgery, to the weeds and beetles and fungus that lessened the melon crop each year. The father never worried about anything. The father was a slothful, languid, easy-smiling drinker. He had remarkable capacity for alcohol.

There was another gift the father had. The father could play the piano. He claimed he'd been a child prodigy. Of course, no one believed him. But at times, sitting at the ancient upright in the shabby, carpetless parlor, he did some startling things with the keyboard.

At other times, when he felt in the mood, he'd give music lessons to five-year-old Edward. It seemed there was nothing else to do with Edward, who was on the quiet side, who stayed away from his villainous brothers as though his very life depended on it. Actually, this was far from the case. They never bullied him. They'd tease him now and then, but they left him alone. They didn't even know he was around. The father felt a little sorry for Edward, who wandered through the house like some lost creature from the woods that had gotten in by mistake.

The music lessons increased from once a week to twice a week and finally to every day. The father became aware that something was happening here, something really unusual. When Edward was nine he performed for a gathering of teachers at the schoolhouse six miles away. When he was fourteen, some people came from Philadelphia to hear him play. They took him back to Philadelphia, to a scholarship at the Curtis Institute of Music.

At nineteen, he gave his first concert in a small auditorium. There wasn't much of an audience, and most of them got in on complimentary tickets. But one of them was a man from New York, a concert artists' manager, and his name was Eugene Alexander.

Alexander had his office on Fifty-seventh Street, not many doors away from Carnegie Hall. It was a small office and the list of clients was rather small. But the furnishings of the office were extremely expensive, and the clients were all big names or on their way to becoming big names. When Edward signed with Alexander, he was given to understand that he was just a tiny drop of water in a very large pool. "And frankly," Alexander said, "I must tell you of the obstacles in this field. In this field the competition is ferocious, downright ferocious. But if you're willing to—"

He was more than willing. He was bright-eyed and anxious to get started. He started the very next day, studying under Gelensky, with Alexander paying for the lessons. Gelensky was a sweetly-smiling little man, completely bald, his face criss-crossed with so many wrinkles that he looked like a goblin. And, as Edward soon learned, the sweet smiles were more on the order of goblin's smiles, concealing a fiendish tendency to ignore the fact that the fingers are flesh and bone, that the fingers can get tired. "You must never get tired," the little man would say, smiling sweetly. "When the hands begin to sweat, that's good. The flow of sweat is the stream of attainment."

He sweated plenty. There were nights when his fingers were so stiff that he felt as though he was wearing splints. Nights when his eyes were seared with the strain of seven and eight and nine hours at the keyboard, the notes on the music sheets finally blurring to a gray mist. And nights of self-doubt, of discouragement. Is it worth all this? he'd ask himself. It's work, work, and more work. And so much work ahead. So much to learn. Oh, Christ, this is hard, it's really hard. It's being cooped up in this room all the time, and even if you wanted to go out, you couldn't. You're too tired. But you ought to get out. For some fresh air, at least. Or a walk in Central Park; it's nice in Central Park. Yes, but there's no piano in Central Park. The piano is here, in this room.

It was a basement apartment on Seventy-sixth Street between Amsterdam and Columbus Avenues. The rent was fifty dollars a month and the rent money came from Alexander. The money for food and clothes and all incidentals also came from Alexander. And for the piano. And for the radio-phonograph, along with several albums of concertos and sonatas. Everything was from Alexander.

Will he get it back? Edward asked himself. Do I have what he thinks I have? Well, we'll soon find out. Not really soon, though. Gelensky is certainly taking his time. He hasn't even mentioned your New York debut. You've been with Gelensky almost two years now and he hasn't said a word about a concert. Or even a small recital. What does that mean? Well, you can ask him. That is, if you're not afraid to ask him. But I think you're afraid. Coming right down to it, I think you're afraid he'll say yes, and then comes the test, the real test here in New York.

Because New York is not Philadelphia. These New York critics are so much tougher. Look what they did last week to Harbenstein. And Gelensky had Harbenstein for five years. Another thing, Harbenstein is managed by Alexander. Does that prove something?

It could. It very well could. It could prove that despite a superb teacher and a devoted, efficient manager, the performer just didn't have it, just couldn't make the grade. Poor Harbenstein. I wonder what Harbenstein did the next day when he read the write-ups? Cried, probably. Sure, he cried. Poor devil. You wait so long for that one chance, you aim your hopes so high, and next thing you know it's all over and they've ripped you apart, they've slaughtered you. But what I think now, you're getting jumpy. And that's absurd, Edward. There's certainly no reason to be jumpy. Your name is Edward Webster Lynn and you're a concert pianist, you're an artist.

Three weeks later he was told by Gelensky that he'd soon be making his New York debut. In the middle of the following week, in Alexander's office, he signed a contract to give a recital. It was to be a one-hour recital in the small auditorium of a small art museum on upper Fifth Avenue. He went back to the little basement apartment, dizzily excited and elated, and saw the envelope, and opened it, and stood there staring at the mimeographed notice. It was from Washington. It ordered him to report to his local draft board.

They classified him 1-A. They were in a hurry and there was no use preparing for the recital. He went to South Jersey, spent a day with his parents, who informed him that Clifton had been wounded in the Pacific and Turley was somewhere in the Aleutians with the Seabees. His mother gave him a nice dinner and his father forced him to have a drink "for good luck." He went back to New York, then to a training camp in Missouri, and from there he was sent to Burma.

He was with Merrill's Marauders. He got hit three times. The first time it was shrapnel in the leg. Then it was a bullet in the shoulder. The last time it was multiple bayonet wounds in the ribs and abdomen, and in the hospital they doubted that he'd make it. But he was very anxious to make it. He was thinking in terms of getting back to New York, to the piano, to the night when he'd put on a white tie and face the audience at Carnegie Hall.

When he returned to New York, he was informed that Alexander had died of kidney trouble and a university in

Chile had given Gelensky an important professorship. They're really gone? he asked the Manhattan sky and streets as he walked alone and felt the ache of knowing it was true, that they were really gone. It meant he had to start all over.

Well, let's get started. First thing, we find a concert manager.

He couldn't find a manager. Or, rather, the managers didn't want him. Some were polite, some were kind and said they wished they could do something but there were so many pianists, the field was so crowded—

And some were blunt, some were downright brutal. They didn't even bother to write his name on a card. They made him acutely aware of the fact that he was unknown, a nobody.

He went on trying. He told himself it couldn't go on this way, and sooner or later he'd get a chance, there'd be at least one sufficiently interested to say, "All right, try some Chopin. Let's hear you play Chopin."

But none of them was interested, not the least bit interested. He wasn't much of a salesman. He couldn't talk about himself, couldn't get it across that Eugene Alexander had come to that first recital, had signed him onto a list that included some of the finest, and that Gelensky had said, "No, they won't applaud. They'll sit there stupefied. The way you're playing now, you are a master of pianoforte. You think there are many? In this world, according to my latest count, there are nine. Exactly nine."

He couldn't quote Gelensky. There were times when he tried to describe his own ability, his full awareness of this talent he had, but the words wouldn't come out. The talent was all in the fingers and all he could say was, "If you'd let me play for you—"

They brushed him off.

It went on like that for more than a year while he worked at various jobs. He was a shipping clerk and truck driver and construction laborer, and there were other jobs that lasted for only a few weeks or a couple of months. It wasn't because he was lazy, or tardy, or lacked the muscle. When they fired him, they said it was mostly "forgetfulness" or "absent-mindedness" or some of them, more perceptive, would comment, "you're only half here; you got your thoughts someplace else."

But the Purple Heart with two clusters started paying off and the disability money was enough to get him a larger room, and then an apartment, and finally an apartment just about big enough to label it a studio. He bought a piano on the installment plan, and put out a sign that stated simply, Piano Teacher.

Fifty cents a lesson. They couldn't afford more. They were mostly Puerto Ricans who lived in the surrounding tenements in the West Nineties. One of them was a girl named Teresa Fernandez, who worked nights behind the counter of a tiny fruit-drink enterprise near Times Square. She was nineteen years old, and a war widow. His name had been Luis and he'd been blown to bits on a heavy cruiser during some action in the Coral Sea. There were no children and now she lived alone in a fourth-floor-front on Ninety-third Street. She was a quiet girl, a diligent and per-severing music student, and she had no musical talent whatsoever.

After several lessons, he saw the way it was, and he told her to stop wasting the money. She said she didn't care about the money, and if Meester Leen did not mind she would be most grateful to take more lessons. Maybe with some more lessons I will start to learn something. I know I am stupid, but—

"Don't say that," he told her. "You're not stupid at all. It's just—"

"I like dese lessons, Meester Leen. It is a nice way for me to pass the time in dese afternoons."

"You really like the piano?"

"Yes, yes. Very much." A certain eagerness that glowed in her eyes, and he knew what it was, he knew it had nothing to do with music. She looked away, blinking hard and try-ing to cover up, and then bit her lip, as though to scold her-self for letting it show. She was embarrassed and silently apologetic, her shoulders drooping just a little, her slender throat twitching as she swallowed the words she didn't dare to let out. He told himself she was something very pleasant, very sweet, and, also, she was lonely. It was apparent that she was terribly lonely.

Her features and her body were on the fragile side, and she had a graceful way of moving. Her looks were more Castilian than Caribbean. Her hair was a soft-hued amber, her eyes were amber, and her complexion was pearl-white, the kind of complexion they try to buy in the expensive salons. Teresa had it from someone down the line a very long time ago, before they'd come over from Spain. There was a trace of deep-rooted nobility in the line of her lips and in the coloring of them. Yes, this is something real, he decided, and wondered why he'd never noticed it before. Until this moment she'd been just another girl who wanted to learn piano.

Three months later they were married. He took her to South Jersey to meet his family, and prepared her for it with a frank briefing, but it turned out to be pleasant in South Jersey. It was especially pleasant because the brothers weren't there to make a lot of noise and lewd remarks. Clifton was presently engaged in some kind of work that required him to do considerable traveling. Turley was a longshoreman on the Philadelphia waterfront. They hadn't been home for more than a year. Once every few months there'd be a post card from Turley, but nothing from Clifton, and the mother said to Teresa, "He ought to write, at least. Don't you think he ought to write?" It was as though Teresa had been a member of the family for years. They were at the table and the mother had roasted a goose. It was a very special dinner and the father made it extra-special by appearing with combed hair, a clean shirt, and scrubbed fingernails. And all day long he'd stayed off the liquor. But after dinner he was at it again and within a few hours he'd consumed the better part of a quart. He winked at Teresa and said, "Say, you're one hell of a pretty girl. Come over here and gimme a kiss." She smiled at her father-in-law and said, "To celebrate the happiness?" and went to him and gave him a kiss. He took another drink from the bottle and winked at Edward and said, "You got yourself a sweet little number here. Now what you wanna do is hold onto her. That New York's a fast town—"

They went back to the basement apartment on Ninety-third Street. He continued giving piano lessons, and Teresa remained at the fruit-drink stand. Some weeks passed, and then he asked her to quit the job. He said he didn't like this nightwork routine. It was a locale that worried him, he explained, stating that although she'd never had trouble with Times Square night owls, it was nevertheless a possibility.

"But is always policemen around there," she argued. "The policemen, they protect the women—"

"Even so," he said, "I can think of safer places than Times Square late at night."

"Like what places?"

"Well, like—"

"Like here? With you?"

He mumbled, "Whenever you're not around, it's like—well, it's like I'm blindfolded."

"You like to see me all the time? You need me that much?"

He touched his lips to her forehead. "It's more than that. It's so much more—"

"I know," she breathed, and held him tightly. "I know what you mean. Is same with me. Is more each day—"

She quit the Times Square job, and found nine-to-five employment in a coffee shop on Eighty-sixth Street off Broadway. It was a nice little place, with a generally pleasant atmosphere, and some days he'd go there for lunch. They'd play a game, customer-and-waitress, pretending that they didn't know each other, and he'd try to make a date. Then one day, after she'd worked there for several months, they were playing the customer-waitress game and he was somehow aware of an interruption, a kind of intrusion.

It was a man at a nearby table. The man was watching them, smiling at them. At her? he wondered, and gazed levelly at the man. But then it was all right and he said to himself, It's me, he's smiling at me. As if he knows me—

Then the man stood up and came over and introduced himself. His name was Woodling. He was a concert manager and of course he remembered Edward Webster Lynn. "Yes, of course," Woodling said, as Edward gave his name, "you came to my office about a year ago. I was terribly busy then and couldn't give you much time. I'm sorry if I was rather abrupt—"

"Oh, that's all right. I understand the way it is."

"It shouldn't be that way," Woodling said. "But this is such a frantic town, and there's so much competition."

Teresa said, "Would the gentlemen like to have lunch?"

Her husband smiled at her, took her hand. He introduced her to Woodling, then explained the customer-waitress game. Woodling laughed and said it was a wonderful game, there were always two winners.

"You mean we both get the prize?" Teresa asked.

"Especially the customer," Woodling said, gesturing toward Edward. "He's a very fortunate man. You're really a prize, my dear."

"Thank you," Teresa murmured. "Is very kind of you to say."

Woodling insisted on paying for the lunch. He invited the pianist to visit him at his office. They made an appointment for an afternoon meeting later that week. When Woodling walked out of the coffee shop, the pianist sat there with his mouth open just a little. "What is it?" Teresa asked, and he said, "Can't believe it. Just can't—"

"He gives you a job?"

"Not a job. It's a chance. I never thought it would happen. I'd given up hoping."

"This is something important?"

He nodded very slowly.

Three days later he entered the suite of offices on Fifty-seventh Street. The furnishings were quietly elegant, the rooms large. Woodling's private office was very large, and featured several oil paintings. There was a Matisse and a Picasso and some by Utrillo.

They had a long talk. Then they went into an audition room and Edward seated himself at a mahogany Baldwin. He played some Chopin, some Schumann, and an extremely difficult piece by Stravinsky. He was at the piano for exactly forty-two minutes. Woodling said, "Excuse me a moment," and walked out of the room, and came back with a contract.

It was a form contract and it offered nothing in the way of guarantees. It merely stipulated that for a period of not less than three years the pianist would be managed and represented by Arthur Woodling. But this in itself was like starting the climb up a gem-studded ladder. In the field of classical music, the name Woodling commanded instant attention from coast to coast, from hemisphere to hemisphere. He was one of the biggest.

Woodling was forty-seven. He was of medium height and built leanly and looked as though he took very good care of himself. He had a healthy complexion. His eyes were clear and showed that he didn't go in for overwork or excessively late hours. He had a thick growth of tightly-curled black hair streaked with white and at the temples it was all white. His features were neatly sculptured, except for the left side of his jaw. It was slightly out of line, the souvenir of a romantic interlude some fifteen years before when a coloratura-soprano had ended their relationship during a South American concert tour. She'd used a heavy bronze book-end to fracture his jaw.

On the afternoon of the contract-signing ceremony with Edward Webster Lynn, the concert manager wore a stiffly starched white collar and a gray cravat purchased in Spain. His suit was also from Spain. His cuff links were emphatically Spanish, oblongs of silver engraved with conquistador helmets. The Spanish theme, especially the cuff links, had been selected specifically for this occasion.

Seven months later, Edward Webster Lynn made his New York debut. It was at Carnegie Hall. They shouted for encores. Next it was Chicago, and then New York again. And after his first coast-to-coast tour they wanted him in Europe.

In Europe he had them leaping to their feet, crying "bravo" until their voices cracked. In Rome the women threw flowers onto the stage. When he came back to Carnegie Hall the seats had been sold out three months in advance. During that year when he was twenty-five, he gave four performances at Carnegie Hall.

In November of that year, he played at the Academy of Music in Philadelphia. He performed the Grieg *Concerto* and the audience was somewhat hysterical, some of them were sobbing, and a certain critic became incoherent and finally speechless. Later that night, Woodling gave a party in his suite at the Town-Casa. It was on the fourth floor. At a few minutes past midnight, Woodling came over to the pianist and said, "Where's Teresa?"

"She said she was tired."

"Again?"

"Yes." He said it quietly. "Again."

Woodling shrugged. "Perhaps she doesn't like these parties."

The pianist lit a cigarette. He held it clumsily. A waiter approached with a tray and glasses of champagne. The pianist reached for a glass, changed his mind and pulled tightly at the cigarette. He jetted the smoke from between his teeth, looked down at the floor and said, "It isn't the parties, Arthur. She's tired all the time. She's—"

There was another stretch of quiet. Then Woodling said, "What is it? What's the matter?"

The pianist didn't answer.

"Perhaps the strain of traveling, living in hotels—"

"No." He said it somewhat harshly. "It's me."

"Quarrels?"

"I wish it were quarrels. This is something worse. Much worse."

"You care to talk about it?" Woodling asked.

"That won't help."

Woodling took his arm and led him out of the room, away from the array of white ties and evening gowns. They went into a smaller room. They were alone there, and Woodling said, "I want you to tell me. Tell me all of it."

"It's a personal matter—"

"You need advice, Edward. I can't advise you unless you tell me."

The pianist looked down at the smoking cigarette stub. He felt the fire near his fingers. He moved toward a table, mashed the stub in an ashtray, turned and faced the concert manager. "She doesn't want me."

"Now, really—"

"You don't believe it? I didn't believe it, either. I couldn't believe it."

"Edward, it's impossible."

"Yes, I know. That's what I've been telling myself for months." And then he shut his eyes tightly, gritting it, "For months? It's been more than a year—"

"Sit down."

He fell into a chair. He stared at the floor and said, "It

started slowly. At first it was hardly noticeable, as though she were trying to hide it. Like—like fighting something. Then gradually it showed itself. I mean, we'd be talking and she'd turn away and walk out of the room. It got to the point where I'd try to open the door and the door was locked. I'd call to her and she wouldn't answer. And the way it is now—well, it's over with, that's all."

"Has she told you?"

"Not in so many words."

"Then maybe—"

"She's sick? No, she isn't sick. That is, it isn't a sickness they can treat. If you know what I mean."

"I know what you mean, but I still can't believe—"

"She doesn't want me, Arthur. She just doesn't want me, that's all."

Woodling moved toward the door.

"Where are you going?" the pianist asked.

"I'm getting you a drink."

"I don't want a drink."

"You'll have one," Woodling said. "You'll have a double."

The concert manager walked out of the room. The pianist sat bent over, his face cupped in his hands. He stayed that way for some moments. Then he straightened abruptly and got to his feet. He was breathing hard.

He went out of the room, down the hall toward the stairway. Their suite was on the seventh floor. He went up the three flights with a speed that had him breathless as he entered the living room.

He called her name. There was no answer. He crossed the parlor to the bedroom door. He tried it, and it was open.

She was sitting on the edge of the bed, wearing a robe. In her lap was a magazine. It was open but she wasn't looking at it. She was looking at the wall.

"Teresa—"

She went on looking at the wall.

He moved toward her. He said, "Get dressed."

"What for?"

"The party," he said. "I want you there at the party."

She shook her head.

"Teresa, listen—"

"Please go." she said. She was still looking at the wall. She raised a hand and gestured toward the door. "Go—"

"No," he said. "Not this time."

Then she looked at him. "What?" Her eyes were dull. "What did you say?"

"I said not this time. This time we talk it over. We find out what it's all about."

"There is nothing—"

"Stop that," he cut in. He moved closer to her. "I've had enough of that. The least you can do is tell me—"

"Why you shout? You never shout at me. Why you shout now?"

"I'm sorry." He spoke in a heavy whisper. "I didn't mean to—"

"Is all right." She smiled at him. "You have right to shout. You have much right."

"Don't say that." He was turning away, his head lowered.

He heard her saying, "I make you unhappy, no? Is bad for me to do that. Is something I try not to do, but when it is dark you cannot stop the darkness—"

"What's that?" He turned stiffly, staring at her. "What did you mean by that?"

"I mean—I mean." But then she was shaking her head, again looking at the wall. "All the time is darkness. Gets darker. No way to see where to go, what to do."

She's trying to tell me something, he thought. She's trying so hard, but she can't tell me. Why can't she tell me?

She said, "I think there is one thing to do. Only one thing."

He felt coldness in the room.

"I say good-by. I go away—"

"Teresa, please—"

She stood up and moved toward the wall. Then she turned and faced him. She was calm. It was an awful calmness. Her voice was a hollow, toneless semi-whisper as she said, "All right, I tell you—"

"Wait." He was afraid now.

"Is proper that you should know," she said. "Is always proper to give the explanation. To make confession."

"Confession?"

"I did bad thing—"

He winced.

"Was very bad. Was terrible mistake." And then a certain brightness came into her eyes. "But now you are famous pianist, and for that I am glad."

This isn't happening, he told himself. It can't be happening.

"Yes, for that I am glad I did it," she said. "To get you the chance you wanted. Was only one way to get you that chance, to put you in Carnegie Hall."

There was a hissing sound. It was his own breathing.

"Woodling," she said.

He shut his eyes very tightly.

"Was the same week when he signed you to his contract," she went on. "Was a few days later. He comes to the coffee shop. But not for coffee. Not for lunch."

There was another hissing sound. It was louder.

"For business proposition." she said.

I've got to get out of here, he told himself. I can't listen to this.

"At first, when he tells me, is like a puzzle, too much for me. I ask him what he is talking about, and he looks at me as if to say, You don't know? You think about it and you will know. So I think about it. That night I get no sleep. Next day he is there again. You know how a spider works? A spider, he is slow and careful—"

He couldn't look at her.

"—like pulling me away from myself. Like the spirit is one thing and the body is another. Was not Teresa who went with him. Was only Teresa's body. As if I was not there, really. I was with you, I was taking you to Carnegie Hall."

And now it was just a record playing, the narrator's voice giving supplementary details. "—in the afternoons. During my time off. He rented a room near the coffee shop. For weeks, in the afternoons, in that room. And then one night you tell me the news, you have signed the paper to play in Carnegie Hall. When he comes next time to the coffee shop he is just another customer. I hand him the menu and he gives the order. And I think to myself, Is ended, I am me again. Yes, now I can be me.

"But you know, it is a curious thing—what you do yesterday is always part of what you are today. From others you try to hide it. For yourself it is no use trying, it is a kind of mirror, always there. So I look, and what do I see? Do I see Teresa? Your Teresa?

"Is no Teresa in the mirror. Is no Teresa anywhere now. Is just a used-up rag, something dirty. And that is why I have not let you touch me. Or even come close. I could not let you come close to this dirt."

He tried to look at her. He said to himself, Yes, look at her. And go to her. And bow, or kneel. It calls for that, it surely does. But—

His eyes aimed at the door, and beyond the door, and there was fire in his brain. He clenched his teeth, and his hands became stone hammerheads. Every fibre in his body was coiled, braced for the lunge that would take him out of here and down the winding stairway to the fourth-floor suite.

And then, for just a moment, he groped for a segment of control, of discretion. He said to himself, Think now, try to think. If you go out that door she'll see you going away, she'll be here alone. You mustn't leave her here alone.

It didn't hold him. Nothing could hold him. He moved slowly toward the door.

"Edward—"

But he didn't hear. All he heard was a low growl from his own mouth as he opened the door and went out of the bedroom.

Then he was headed across the living room, his arm extended, his fingers clawing at the door leading to the outer hall. In the instant that his fingers touched the door handle, he heard the noise from the bedroom.

It was a mechanical noise. It was the rattling of the chain-pulleys at the sides of the window.

He pivoted and ran across the living room and into the bedroom. She was climbing out. He leaped, and made a grab, but there was nothing to grab. There was just the cold empty air coming in through the wide-open window.

On Front Street, as he stood on the pavement near the red-and-gold entrance to the five-and-dime, the Saturday shoppers swept past him. Some of them bumped him with their shoulders. Others pushed him aside. He was insensible. He wasn't there, really. He was very far away from there.

He was at the funeral seven years ago, and then he was wandering around New York City. It was a time of no direction, no response to traffic signals or changes in the weather. He never knew or cared what hour of the day it was, what day of the week it was. For the sum of everything was a circle, and the circle was labeled Zero.

He had pulled all his savings from the bank. It amounted to about nine thousand dollars. He managed to lose it. He wanted to lose it. The night he lost it, when it was taken from him, he got himself beaten. He wanted that, too. When it happened, when he went down with the blood spilling from his nose and mouth and the gash in his skull, he was glad. He actually enjoyed it.

It happened very late at night, in Hell's Kitchen. Three of them jumped him. One of them had a length of lead pipe. The other two had brass knuckles. The lead pipe came first. It hit him on the side of his head and he walked sideways, then slowly sat down on the curb. Then the others went to work with the brass knuckles. Then something happened. They weren't sure what it was, but it seemed like propeller blades churning the air and coming at them. The one with the lead pipe had made a rapid departure, and they wondered why he wasn't there to help them. They really needed help. One of them went down with four teeth flying out of his mouth. The other was sobbing, "gimme a break, aw, please—gimme a break," and the wild man grinned and whispered, "Fight back—fight back—don't spoil the fun." The thug knew then he had no choice, and did what he could with the brass knuckles and his weight. He had considerable weight. Also, he was quite skilled in the dirtier tactics. He used a knee, he used his thumbs, and he even tried using his teeth. But he just wasn't fast enough. He ended up with both eyes swollen shut, a fractured nose, and a brain concussion. As he lay there on the pavement, flat on his back and unconscious, the wild man whispered, "Thanks for the party."

A few nights later, there was another party. It took place in Central Park when two policemen found the wild man sleeping under a bush. They woke him up, and he told them to go away and leave him alone. They pulled him to his feet, asked him if he had a home. He didn't answer. They started to shoot questions at him. Again he told them to leave him alone. One of them snarled at him and shoved him. The other policeman grabbed his arm. He said, "Let go, please let go." Then they both had hold of him, and they were pulling him along. They were big men and he had to look up at them as he said, "Why don't you leave me alone?" They told him to shut up. He tried to pull loose and one of them hit him on the leg with a night stick. "You hit me," he said. The policeman barked at him, "Sure I hit you. If I want to, I'll hit you again." He shook his head slowly and said, "No, you won't." A few minutes later the two policemen were alone there. One of them was leaning against a tree, breathing hard. The other was sitting on the grass, groaning.

And then, less than a week later, it was in the Bowery and a well known strong-arm specialist remarked through puffed and bleeding lips, "Like stickin' me face in a concrete mixer."

From someone in the crowd, "You gonna fight him again?"

"Sure I'll fight him again. Just one thing I need."

"What?"

"An automatic rifle," the plug-ugly said, sitting there on the curb and spitting blood. "Buy me one of them rifles and keep him a distance."

He was always on the move, roaming from the Bowery to the Lower East Side and up through Yorkville to Spanish Harlem and down and over to Brooklyn, to the brawling grounds of Greenpoint and Brownsville—to any area where a man who looked for trouble was certain to find it.

Now, looking back on it, he saw the wild man of seven years ago, and thought, What it amounted to, you were crazy, I mean really crazy. Call it horror-crazy. With your fingers, that couldn't touch the keyboard or get anywhere near a keyboard, a set of claws, itching to find the throat of the very dear friend and counselor, that so kind and generous man who took you into Carnegie Hall.

But, of course, you knew you mustn't find him. You had to keep away from him, for to catch even a glimpse of him would mean a killing. But the wildness was there, and it needed an outlet. So let's give a vote of thanks to the hooligans, all the thugs and sluggers and roughnecks who were only too happy to accommodate you, to offer you a target.

What about money? It stands to reason you needed money. You had to put food in your belly. Let's see now, I remember there were certain jobs, like dishwashing and polishing cars and distributing handbills. At times you were out of a job, so the only thing to do was hold out your hand and wait for coins to drop in. Just enough nickels and dimes to get you a bowl of soup and a mattress in a flophouse. Or sometimes a roll of gauze to bandage the bleeding cuts. There were nights when you dripped a lot of blood, especially the nights when you came out second best.

Yes, my good friend, you were in great shape in those days. What I think is, you were a candidate for membership in some high-off-the-ground clubhouse. But it couldn't go on like that. It had to stop somewhere. What stopped it?

Sure, it was that trip you took. The stroll that sent you across the bridge into Jersey, a pleasant little stroll of some hundred-and-forty miles. If I remember correctly, it took you the better part of a week to get there, to the house hidden in the woods of South Jersey.

It was getting on toward Thanksgiving. You were coming home to spend the holiday with the folks. They were all there. Clifton and Turley were home for the holiday too. At least, they said that was the reason they'd come home. But after a few drinks they kind of got around to the real reason. They said there'd been some complications, and the authorities were looking for them, and this place deep in the woods was far away from all the guideposts.

The way it was, Turley had quit his job on the Philly waterfront and had teamed up with Clifton on a deal involving stolen cars, driving the cars across state lines. They'd been spotted and chased. Not that it worried them. You remember Clifton saying, "Yeah, it's a tight spot, all right. But we'll get out of it. We always get out of it." And then he laughed, and Turley laughed, and they went on drinking and started to tell dirty jokes. . . .

That was quite a holiday. I mean, the way it ended it was really something. I remember Clifton said something about your situation, your status as a widower. You asked him not to talk about it. He went on talking about it. He winked at Turley and he said to you, "What's it like with a Puerto Rican?"

You smiled at Clifton, you winked at Turley, and you said to your father and mother, "It's gonna be crowded in here. You better go into the next room—"

So then it was you and Clifton, and the table got knocked over, and a couple chairs got broken. It was Clifton on the floor, spitting blood and saying, "What goes on here?" Then he shook his head. He just couldn't believe it. He said to Turley, "Is that really him?"

Turley couldn't answer. He just stood staring.

Clifton got up and went down and got up again. He was all right, he could really take it. You went on knocking him down and he got up and finally he said, "I'm gettin' tired of this." He looked at Turley and muttered, "Take him off me—"

I remember Turley moving in and reaching out and then it was Turley sitting on the floor next to Clifton. It was Clifton laughing and saying, "You here too?" and Turley nodded solemnly and then he got up. He said, "Tell you what I'll do. I'll give you fifty to one you can't do that again."

Then he moved in. He came in nice and easy, weaving. You threw one and missed and then he threw one and his money was safe. You were out for some twenty minutes. And later we were gathered at the table again, and Clifton was grinning and saying, "It figures now, you're slated for the game."

You didn't quite get that. You said, "Game? What game?"

"Our game." He pointed to himself and Turley. "I'm gonna deal you in."

"No," Turley said. "He ain't for the racket."

"He's perfect for the racket," Clifton said quietly and thoughtfully. "He's fast as a snake. He's hard as iron—"

"That ain't the point," Turley cut in. "The point is—"

"He's ready for it, that's the point. He's geared for action."

"He is?" Turley's voice was tight now. "Let him say it, then. Let him say what he wants."

Then it was quiet at the table. They were looking at you, waiting. You looked back at them, your brothers—the heist artists, the gunslingers, the all-out trouble-eaters.

And you thought, Is this the answer? Is this what you're slated for? Well, maybe so. Maybe Clifton has you tagged, with your hands that can't make music any more making cash the easy way. With a gun. You know they use guns. You braced for that? You hard enough for that?

Well, you were hard enough in Burma. In Burma you did plenty with a gun.

But this isn't Burma. This is a choice. Between what? The dirty and the clean? The bad and the good?

Let's put it another way. What's the payoff for the clean ones? The good ones? I mean the ones who play it straight. What do they get at the cashier's window?

Well, friends, speaking from experience, I'd say the payoff is anything from a kick in the teeth to the longbladed scissors slicing in deep and cutting up that pump in your chest. And that's too much, that does it. With all feeling going out and the venom coming in. So then you're saying to the world, All right, you wanna play it dirty, we'll play it dirty.

But no, you were thinking. You don't want that. You join this Clifton-Turley combine, it's strictly on the vicious side and you've had enough of that.

"Well?" Clifton was asking. "What'll it be?"

You were shaking your head. You just didn't know. And then you happened to look up. You saw the other two faces, the older faces. Your mother was shrugging. Your father was wearing the soft-easy smile.

And that was it. That was the answer.

"Well?" from Clifton.

You shrugged. You smiled.

"Come on," Clifton said. "Let's have it."

"He's telling you," from Turley. "Look at his face."

Clifton looked. He took a long look. He said, "It's like—like he's skipped clear outa the picture. As if he just don't care."

"That just about says it," Turley grinned.

Just about. For then and there it was all connections split, it was all issues erased. No venom now, no frenzy, no trace of the wild man in your eyes. The wild man was gone, annihilated by two old hulks who didn't know they were still in there pitching, the dull-eyed, shrugging mother and the easy-smiling, booze-guzzling father.

Without sound you said to them, Much obliged, folks.

And later, when you went away, when you walked down the path that bordered the watermelon patch, you kept thinking it, Much obliged, much obliged.

The path was bumpy, but you didn't feel the bumps. In the woods the narrow, twisting road was deeply rutted, but you sort of floated past the ridges and the chug holes. You remember it was wet-cold in the woods, and there was a blasting wind, but all you felt was a gentle breeze.

You made it through the woods, and onto another road, and still another road, and finally the wide concrete highway that took you into the tiny town and the bus depot. In the depot there was a lush talking loud. He was trying to start something. When he tried with you, it was just no use, he got nowhere. You gave him the shrug, you gave him the smile. It was easy, the way you handled him. Well, sure, it was easy, it was just that nothing look—with your tongue in your cheek.

You took the first bus out. It was headed for Philadelphia. I think it was a few nights later you were in a mid-city gin-mill, one of them fifteen-cents-a-shot establishments. It had a kitchen, and you got a job washing dishes and cleaning the floor and so forth. There was an old wreck of a piano, and you'd look at it, and look away, and look at it again. One night you said to the bartender, "Okay if I play it?"

"You?"

"I think I can play it."

"All right, give it a try. But it better be music."

You sat down at the piano. You looked at the keyboard. And then you looked at your hands.

"Come on," the bartender said. "Watcha waitin' for?"

You lifted your hands. You lowered your hands and your fingers hit the keys.

The sound came out and it was music.

A voice said, "You still here?"

He looked up. The waitress was coming toward him through the crowd of shoppers. She'd emerged from the five-and-dime with a paper bag in her hand. He saw that it was a small bag. He told himself that she hadn't done much shopping.

"How long were you in there?" he asked.

"Just a few minutes."

"Is that all?"

"I got waited on right away," she asked. "All I bought was some toothpaste and a cake of soap. And a toothbrush."

He didn't say anything.

She said, "I didn't ask you to wait for me."

"I wasn't waiting," he said. "I had no place to go, that's all. I was just hanging around."

"Looking at the people?"

"No," he said. "I wasn't looking at the people."

She pulled him away from an oncoming baby carriage. "Come on," she said. "We're blocking traffic."

They moved along with the crowd. The sky was all gray now and getting darker. It was still early in the afternoon, just a little past two, but it seemed much later. People were looking up at the sky and walking faster, wanting to get home before the storm swept in. The threat of it was in the air.

She looked at him. She said, "Button your overcoat."

"I'm not cold."

"I'm freezing," she said. "How far we gotta walk?"

"To Port Richmond? It's a couple miles."

"That's great."

"We could take a taxi, except I haven't got a cent to my name."

"Likewise," she said. "I borrowed four bits from my land-lady and spent it all."

"Well, it ain't too cold for walking."

"The hell it ain't. My toes are coming off."

"We'll walk faster," he said. "That'll keep your feet warm."

They quickened their pace. They were walking with their heads down against the oncoming wind. It was coming harder, whistling louder. It lifted the snow from pavement and street and there were powdery flurries of the tiny flakes. Then larger snowflakes were falling. The air was thick with snow, and it was getting colder.

"Nice day for a picnic," she said. And just then she slipped on some hard-packed snow and was falling back-ward and he grabbed her. Then he slipped and they were both falling but she managed to get a foothold and they stayed on their feet. A store owner was standing in the doorway of his dry-goods establishment, saying to them, "Watch your step out there. It's slippery." She glared at the man and said, "Yeah, we know it's slippery. It wouldn't be slippery if you'd clean the pavement." The store owner grinned and said, "So if you fall, you'll sue me."

The man went back into the store. They stood there on the slippery pavement, still holding onto each other to keep from falling. He said to himself, That's all it amounts to, just holding her so she won't slide and slip and go down. But I guess it's all right now, I guess you can let go.

You better let go, damn it. Because it's there again, it's happening again. You'll hafta stop it, that's all. You can't let it get you like this. It's really getting you and she knows it. Of course she knows. She's looking at you and she—

Say, what's the matter with your arms? Why can't you let go of her? Now look, you'll just hafta stop it.

I think the way to stop it is shrug it off. Or take it with your tongue in your cheek. Sure, that's the system. At any rate it's the system that works for you. It's the automatic control board that keeps you way out there where nothing matters, where it's only you and the keyboard and nothing else. Because it's gotta be that way. You gotta stay clear of anything serious.

You wanna know something? The system just ain't working now. I think it's Eddie giving way to Edward Webster Lynn. No, it can't be that way. We won't let it be that way. Oh, Christ, why'd she have to mention that name? Why'd she have to bring it all back? You had it buried and you were getting along fine and having such a high old time not caring about anything. And now this comes along. This hits you and sets a spark and before we know it there's a fire started. A what? You heard me, I said it's a fire. And here's a flash just came in—it's blazing too high and we can't put it out.

We can't? Check the facts, man, check the facts. This is Eddie here. And Eddie can't feel fire. Eddie can't feel anything.

His arms fell away from her. There was nothing at all in his eyes as he gave her the soft-easy smile. He said, "Let's get moving. We got a long way to go."

She looked at him, and took a slow deep breath, and said, "You're telling me?"

Some forty minutes later they entered Harriet's Hut. The place was jammed. It was always busy on Saturday afternoons, but when the weather was bad the crowd was doubled. Against all snow and blasting wind, the Hut was a fortress and a haven. It was also a fueling station. The bartender rushed back and forth, doing his level best to supply the demand for antifreeze.

Harriet was behind the bar, at the cash register. She spotted the waitress and the piano man, and yapped at them, "Where ya been? What the hell ya think it is, a holiday?"

"Sure it's a holiday," the waitress said. "We don't start work till nine tonight. That's the schedule."

"Not today it ain't," Harriet told her. "Not with a mob like this. You shoulda known I'd need you here. And you," she said to Eddie, "you oughta know the score on this kinda weather. They come in off the street, the place gets filled, and they wanna hear music."

Eddie shrugged. "I got up late."

"Yeah, he got up late," Lena said. She spoke very slowly with a certain deliberation. "Then we went for a ride. And then we took a walk."

Harriet frowned. "Together?"

"Yeah," she said. "Together."

The Hut owner looked at the piano man. "What's the wire on that?"

He didn't answer. The waitress said, "Whatcha want him to do, make a full report?"

"If he wants to," Harriet said, still looking quizzically at the piano man. "It's just that I'm curious, that's all. He usually walks alone."

"Yeah, he's a loner, all right," the waitress murmured. "Even when he's with someone, he's alone."

Harriet scratched the back of her neck. "Say, what goes on here? What's all this who-struck-John routine?"

"You get the answer on page three," the waitress said. "Except there ain't no page three."

"Thanks," Harriet said. "That helps a lot." Then, abruptly she yelled, "Look, don't stand there giving me puzzles. I don't need puzzles today. Just put on your apron and get to work."

"First we get paid."

"We?" Harriet was frowning again.

"Well, me, anyway," the waitress said. "I want a week's wages and three in advance for this extra time today."

"What's the rush?"

"No rush." Lena pointed to the cash register. "Just take it out nice and slow and hand it to me."

"Later," the fat blonde said. "I'm too busy now."

"Not too busy to gimme my salary. And while you're at it, you can pay him, too. You want him to make music, you pay him."

Eddie shrugged. "I can wait—"

"You'll stay right here and get your money," Lena cut in. And then, to Harriet, "Come on, dish out the greens."

For a long moment Harriet didn't move. She stood there studying the face of the waitress. Then, with a backward gesture of her hand, as though to cast something over her shoulder to get it out of the way, she turned her attention to the cash register.

It's all right now, Eddie thought. It was tight there for a minute but I think it's all right now. He ventured a side glance at the expressionless face of the waitress. If only she leaves it alone, he said to himself. It don't make sense to start with Harriet. With Harriet it's like starting with dynamite. Or maybe that's what she wants. Yes, I think she's all coiled up inside, she's craving some kind of explosion.

Harriet was taking money from the cash register, counting out the bills and jutting them in Lena's palm. She finished paying Lena and turned to the piano man, putting the money on the bar in front of him. As she placed some ones on top of the fives, she was muttering, "Ain't enough I get grief from the customers. Now the help comes up with labor troubles. All of a sudden they go and form a union."

"That's the trend," the waitress said.

"Yeah?" Harriet said. "Well, I don't like it."

"Then lump it," Lena said.

The fat blonde stopped counting out the money. She blinked a few times. Then she straightened slowly, her immense bosom jutting as she inhaled a vast lungful. "What's that?" she said.

"What'd you say?"

"You heard me."

Harriet placed her hands on her huge hips. "Maybe I didn't hear correct. Because they don't talk to me that way. They know better. I'll tell you something, girl. Ain't a living cat can throw that kinda lip at me and get away with it."

"That so?" Lena murmured.

"Yeah, that's so," Harriet said. "And you're lucky. I'm letting you know it the easy way. Next time it won't be so easy. You sound on me again, you'll get smacked down."

"Is that a warning?"

"Bright red."

"Thanks," Lena said. "Now here's one from me to you. I've been smacked down before. Somehow I've always managed to get up."

"Jesus." Harriet spoke aloud to herself. "What gives with this one here? It's like she's lookin' for it. She's really begging for it."

The waitress stood with her arms loose at her sides. She was smiling now.

Harriet had a thoughtful look on her face. She spoke softly to the waitress. "What's the matter, Lena? What bothers you?"

The waitress didn't answer.

"All right, I'll let it pass," the Hut owner said.

Lena held onto the thin smile. "You don't have to, really."

"I know I don't hafta. But it's better that way. Dontcha think it's better that way?"

The thin smile was aimed at nothing in particular. The waitress said, "Any way it goes all right with me. But don't do me any favors. I don't need no goddam favors from you."

Harriet frowned and slanted her head and said, "You sure you know what you're saying?"

Lena didn't answer.

"Know what I think?" Harriet murmured. "I think you got your people mixed."

Lena lost the smile. She lowered her head. She nodded, then shook her head, then nodded again.

"Ain't that what it is?" Harriet prodded gently.

Lena went on nodding. She looked up at the fat blonde. She said, "Yeah, I guess so." And then, tonelessly, "I'm sorry, Harriet. It's just that I'm bugged about something—I didn't mean to take it out on you."

"What is it?" Harriet asked. The waitress didn't answer. Harriet looked inquiringly at Eddie. The piano man shrugged and didn't say anything. "Come on, let's have it," Harriet demanded. "What is it with her?" He shrugged again and remained quiet. The fat blonde sighed and said, "All right, I give up," and resumed counting out the money. Then the money was all there on the bar and he picked it up and folded the thin roll and let it fall into his overcoat pocket. He turned away from the bar and took a few steps and heard Lena saying, "Wait, I got something for you."

He came back and she handed him two quarters, two dimes and a nickel. "From last night," she said, not looking at him. "Now we're squared."

He looked down at the coins in his hand. Squared, he thought. All squared away. That makes it quits. That ends it. Well, sure, that's the way you want it. That's fine.

But just then he saw she was stiffening, she was staring

at something. He glanced in that direction and saw Wally Plyne coming toward the bar where they stood.

The big-paunched bouncer wore a twisted grin as he approached. His thick shoulders were hunched, weaving in wrestler's style. The grin widened, and Eddie thought, He's forcing it, and what we get next is one of them real friendly hellos, all sugar and syrup.

And then he felt Plyne's big hand on his arm, heard Plyne's gruff voice saying, "Here he is, the crown prince of the eighty-eights. My boy, Eddie."

"Yeah," the waitress said. "Your boy, Eddie."

Plyne didn't seem to hear her. He said to the piano man, "I was lookin' for you. Where you been hiding?"

"He wasn't hiding," the waitress said.

The bouncer tried to ignore her. He went on grinning at Eddie.

The waitress pushed it further. "How could he hide? He didn't have a chance. They knew his address."

Plyne blinked hard. The grin fell away.

It was quiet for some moments. Then Harriet was saying, "Lemme get in on this." She leaned over from behind the bar. "What's cooking here?"

"Something messy," the waitress said. She indicated the bouncer. "Ask your man there. He knows all about it. He stirred it up."

Harriet squinted at Plyne. "Spill," she said.

"Spill what?" The bouncer backed away. "She's talkin' from nowhere. She's dreamin' or somethin'."

The waitress turned and looked at Harriet. "Look, if you don't wanna hear this—"

The fat blonde took a deep breath. She went on looking at Plyne.

"I hope you can take it," the waitress said to her. "After all, you live with this man."

"Not lately." Harriet's voice was heavy. "Lately I ain't hardly been living at all."

The waitress opened her mouth to speak, and Plyne gritted, "Close your head—"

"Close yours," Harriet told him. And then, to the waitress, "All right, let's have it."

"It's what they call a sellout," Lena said. "I got it straight from the customers. They told me they were here this morning. They bought a few drinks and something else."

Eddie started to move away. The waitress reached out and caught his arm and held him there. He shrugged and smiled. His eyes said to the bouncer, It don't bother me, so don't let it bother you.

The waitress went on, "It was two of them. Two ambassadors, but not the good-will type. These were the ugly kind, the kind that can hurt you. Or make you disappear. You get what I'm talking about?"

Harriet nodded dully.

"They were looking for Eddie," the waitress said.

Harriet frowned, "What for?"

"That ain't the point. The point is, they had a car and they had a gun. What they needed was some information. Like finding out his address."

The frown faded from Harriet's face. She gaped at Plyne. "You didn't tell them—"

"He sure as hell did," Lena said.

Harriet winced.

"They gave him a nice tip, too," the waitress said. "They handed him fifty dollars."

"No." It was a groan. Harriet's mouth twisted. She turned her head to keep from looking at the bouncer.

"I don't wanna work here no more," the waitress said. "I'll just stay a few days, until you get another girl."

"Now wait," the bouncer said. "It ain't that bad."

"It ain't?" Lena faced him. "I'll tell you how bad it is. Ever bait a hook for catfish? They go for the stink. What you do is, you put some worms in a can and leave it out in the sun for a week or so. Then open the can and get a whiff. It'll give you an idea of what this smells like."

Plyne swallowed hard. "Look, you got it all wrong—"

And the waitress said, "Now we get the grease."

"Will ya listen?" Plyne whined. "I'm tellin' you they conned me. I didn't know what they were after. I figured they was—"

"Yeah, we know," Lena murmured. "You thought they were census-takers."

The bouncer turned to Eddie. His arms came up in a pleading gesture. "Ain't I your friend?"

"Sure," Eddie said.

"Would I do anything to hurt you?"

"Of course not."

"You hear that?" The bouncer spoke loudly to the two women. "You hear what he says? He knows I'm on his side."

"I think I'm gonna throw up," Harriet said.

But the bouncer went on, "I'm tellin' you they conned me. If I thought they were out to hurt Eddie, I'da—why for Christ's sake, I'da ripped 'em apart. They come in here again, I'll put them through that plate-glass window, one at a time."

A nearby drinker mumbled, "You tell 'em, Hugger."

And from another guzzler, "When the Hugger tells it, he means it."

"You're goddam right I mean it," Plyne said loudly. "I ain't a man who looks for trouble, but if they want it they'll get it." And then, to Eddie, "Dontcha worry, I can handle them gun-punks. They're little. I'm big."

"How big?" the waitress asked.

Plyne grinned at her. "Take a look."

She looked him up and down. "Yeah, it's there, all right," she murmured. "Really huge."

The bouncer was feeling much better now. He widened the grin. "Huge is correct," he said. "And it's solid, too. It's all man."

"Man?" She stretched the word, her mouth twisted. "What I see is slop."

At the bar the drinkers had stopped drinking. They were staring at the waitress.

"It's just slop," she said. She took a step toward the bouncer.

"The only thing big about you is your mouth."

Plyne grunted again. He mumbled, "I don't like that. I ain't gonna take it—"

"You'll take it," she told him. "You'll eat it."

He's eating it, all right, Eddie thought. He's choking on it. Look at him, look what's in the eyes. Because he's getting it from her, that's why. He goes for her so much it's got him all jelly, it's driving him almost loony. And there's nothing he can do about it, except take it. Just stand there and take it. Yes he's getting it, sure enough. I've seen them get it, but not like this.

Now the crowd at the bar was moving in closer. From the tables they were rising and edging forward so as not to miss a word of it. The only sound in the Hut was the voice of the waitress. She spoke quietly, steadily, and what came from her lips was like a blade going into the bouncer.

Really ripping him apart, Eddie thought. Come to think of it, what's happening here is a certain kind of amputation. And we don't mean the arms or the legs.

And look at Harriet. Look what's happening to her. She's aged some ten years in just a few minutes. Her man is getting slashed and chopped. It's happening right in front of her eyes, and there ain't a word she can say, a move she can make. She knows it's true.

Sure, it's true. No getting away from that. The bouncer played it dirty today. But even so, I think he's getting worse than he deserves. You gotta admit, he's had some hard knocks lately, I mean this problem with the waitress, this night after night of seeing it there and wanting it, and knowing there ain't a chance. And even now, while she tears him to pieces, spits on him in front of all these people, he can't take his hungry eyes off her. You gotta feel sorry for the bouncer, it's a sad matinee for the Harleyville Hugger.

Poor Hugger. He wanted so much to make a comeback, some sort of comeback. He thought if he could make it with the waitress, he'd be proving something. Like proving he still had it, the power, the importance, the stuff and the drive, and whatever it takes to make a woman say yes. What he got from the waitress was a cold, silent no. Not even a look.

Well, he's getting something now. He's getting plenty. It's grief in spades, that's what it is. I wish she'd stop it, I think she's pushing it too far. Does she know what she's doing to him? She can't know. If she knew, she'd stop. If I could only tell her—

Tell her what? That the bouncer ain't as bad as he seems? That he's just another has-been who tried to come back and got himself loused up? Sure, that's the way it is but you can't put it that way. You can't sing the blues for Plyne; you can't sing the blues, period. You're too far away from the scene, that's why. You're high up there and way out there where nothing matters.

Then what are you doing standing here? And looking. And listening. Why ain't you there at the piano?

Or maybe you're waiting for something to happen. It figures, the bouncer can't take much more of this. The waitress keeps it up, something's gonna happen, sure as hell.

Well, so what? It don't involve you. Nothing involves you. What you do now is, you shove off. You cruise away from here and over there to the piano.

He started to move, and then couldn't move. The waitress was still holding onto his arm. He gave a pull, his arm came loose, and the waitress looked at him. Her eyes said, You can't check out; you're included.

His soft-easy smile said, Not in this. Not in anything.

Then he was headed toward the piano. He heard the voice of the waitress as she went on talking to Plyne. His legs moved faster. He was in a hurry to sit down at the keyboard, to start making music. That'll do it, he thought. That'll drown out the buzzing. He took off his overcoat and tossed it onto a chair.

"Hey, Eddie." It was from a nearby table. He glanced in that direction and saw the yellow-orange dyed hair, the skinny shoulders and flat chest. The lips of Clarice were gin-wet, and her eyes were gin-shiny. She was sitting there alone, unaware of the situation at the bar.

"C'mere," she said. "C'mere and I'll show you a trick."

"Later," he murmured, and went on toward the piano. But then he thought, That wasn't polite. He turned and smiled at Clarice, and walked over to the table and sat down. "All right," he said. "Let's see it."

She was off her chair and onto the table, attempting a one-armed handstand. She went off the table and landed on the floor.

"Nice try," Eddie said. He reached down and helped her to her feet. She slid back onto the chair. From across the room, from the bar, he could hear the voice of the waitress, still giving it to Plyne. Don't listen, he told himself. Try to concentrate on what Clarice is saying.

Clarice was saying, "You sure fluffed me off last night."

"Well, it just wasn't there."

She shrugged. She reached for a shot glass, picked it up and saw it was empty. With a vague smile at the empty glass she said, "That's the way it goes. If it ain't there, it just ain't there."

"That figures."

"You're damn right it figures." She reached out and gave him an affectionate pat on the shoulder. "Maybe next time—"

"Sure," he said.

"Or maybe—" she lowered the glass to the table and pushed it aside—"maybe there won't be a next time."

"Whatcha mean?" He frowned slightly. "You closing up shop?"

"No," she said. "I'm still in business. I mean you."

"Me? What's with me?"

"Changes," Clarice said. "I gander certain changes."

His frown deepened "Like what?"

"Well, like last night, for instance. And just a little while ago, when you walked in with the waitress. It was—well, I've seen it happen before. I can always tell when it happens."

"When what happens? What're you getting at?"

"The collision," she said. She wasn't looking at him. She was talking to the shot glass and the table top. "That's what it is, a collision. Before they know it, it hits them. They just can't avoid it. Not even this one here, this music man with his real cool style. It was easy-come and easy-go and all of a sudden he gets hit—"

"Say, look, you want another drink?"

"I always want another drink."

He started to get up. "You sure need it now."

She pulled him back onto the chair. "First gimme the low-down. I like to get these facts first hand. Maybe I'll send it to Winchell."

"What is this? You dreaming up something?"

"Could be," Clarice murmured. She looked at him. It was a probing look. "Except it shows. It's scribbled all over your face. It was there when I seen you comin' in with her."

"Her? The waitress?"

"Yeah, the waitress. But she wasn't no cheap-joint waitress then. She was Queen of the Nile and you were that soldier, or something, from Rome."

He laughed. "It's the gin, Clarice. The gin's got you looped."

"You think so? I don't think so." She reached for the empty glass, pulled it toward her on the table. "Let's have a look in the crystal ball," she said.

Her hands were cupped around the shot glass, and she sat there looking intently at the empty jigger.

"I see something," she said.

"Clarice, it's just an empty glass."

"Ain't empty now. There's a cloud. There's shadows—"

"Come off it," he said.

"Quiet," she breathed. "It's comin' closer."

"All right." He grinned. "I'll go along with the gag. Whaddya see in the glass?"

"It's you and the waitress—"

For some reason he closed his eyes. His hands gripped the sides of the chair.

He heard Clarice saying, "—no other people around. Just you and her. It's in the summertime. And there's a beach. There's water—"

"Water?" He opened his eyes, his hands relaxed, and he grinned again. "That ain't water. It's gin. You're swimmin' in it."

Clarice ignored him. She went on gazing at the shot glass. "You both got your clothes on. Then she takes off her clothes. Look what she's doin'. She's all naked."

"Keep it clean," he said.

"You stand there and look at her," Clarice continued. "She runs across the sand. Then she takes a dive in the waves. She tells you to get undressed and come on in, the water's fine. You stand there—"

"That's right," he said. "I just stand there. I don't make a move."

"But she wants you—"

"The hell with her," he said. "That ocean's too deep for me."

Clarice looked at him. Then she looked at the shot glass. Now it was just an empty jigger that needed a refill.

"You see?" he said. And he grinned again. "There ain't nothing happening."

"You leveling? With yourself, I mean."

"Well, if it's proof you need—" He put his hand in his pocket and took out the roll of money, his salary from Harriet. He peeled off three ones and put them on the table. "I'm paying you in advance," he said. "For the next time."

She looked at the three ones.

"Take it," he said. "You might as well take it. You're gonna work for it."

Clarice shrugged and took the money off the table. She slipped the bills under her sleeve. "Well, anyway," she said "it's nice to know you're still my customer."

"Permanent," he said, with the soft-easy smile. "Let's shake on it."

And he put out his hand. Just then he heard the noise from the bar. It was a growl, and then a gasp from the crowd. He turned his head and saw the crowd moving back, shoving and pushing to stay clear of the bouncer. The growl came again, and Harriet was coming out from behind the bar, moving fast as she attempted to step between the bouncer and the waitress. The bouncer shoved her aside. It was a violent shove, and Harriet stumbled and hit the floor sitting down. Then the bouncer let out another growl, and took a slow step toward the waitress. The waitress stood there motionless. Plyne raised his arm. He hesitated, as though he wasn't quite sure what he wanted to do. The waitress smiled thinly, sneeringly, daring him to go through with it. He swung his arm and the flat of his hand cracked hard against her mouth.

Eddie got up from the chair. He walked toward the crowd at the bar.

He was pushing his way through the crowd. They were packed tightly, and he had to use his elbows. As he forced a path, they gasped, for Plyne hit the waitress a second time. This time it was a knuckle smash with the back of the hand.

Eddie kept pushing, making his way through the crowd.

The waitress had not moved. A trickle of red moved slant-wise from her lower lip.

"You'll take it back," the bouncer said. He was breathing very hard. "You'll take back every—"

"Kiss my ass," the waitress said.

Plyne hit her again, with his palm. And then again, with the back of his hand.

Harriet was up from the floor, getting between them. The bouncer grabbed her arm and flung her sideways. She went sailing across the floor, landed heavily on her knees, and then twisted her ankle as she tried to get up. She fell back. She sat there rubbing her ankle, staring at Plyne and the waitress.

The bouncer raised his arm again. "You gonna take it back?"

"No."

His open hand crashed against her face. She reeled against the bar, recovered her balance and stood there, still smiling thinly. Now a thicker stream of blood came from her mouth. One side of her face was welted with finger-marks. The other side was swollen and bruised.

"I'll ruin you," Plyne screamed at her. "I'll make you wish you'd never seen me—"

"I can't see you now," the waitress said. "I can't look down that far."

Plyne hit her again with his palm. Then he clenched his fist.

Eddie was using his arms like scythes, a feeling of desperation on him now.

Plyne said to the waitress, "You're gonna take it back. You'll take it back if I hafta knock all your teeth out."

"That won't do it," the waitress said. She licked at her bleeding lip.

"God damn you." Plyne hissed. He hauled off and swung his fist at her face. His fist was in mid-air when a hand grabbed his arm. He jerked loose and hauled off again. The hand came down on his arm, holding tightly now. He turned his head to see who had interfered.

"Leave her alone," Eddie said.

"You?" the bouncer said again.

Eddie didn't say anything. He was still holding the bouncer's arm. He moved slowly, stepping between Plyne and the waitress.

Plyne's eyes were wide. He was genuinely astonished. "Not Eddie," he said. "Anyone but Eddie."

"All right," the piano man murmured. "Let's break it up."

"Christ," the bouncer said. He turned and gaped at the gaping crowd. "Look what's happenin' here. Look who's tryin' to break it up."

"I mean it, Wally."

"What? You what?" And then again to the crowd, "Get that? He says he means it."

"It's gone far enough," Eddie said.

"Well I'll be—" The bouncer didn't know what to make of it. Then he looked down and saw the hand still gripping his arm. "Whatcha doin'?" he asked, his voice foggy with amazement. "Whatcha think you're doin'?"

Eddie spoke to the waitress. "Take off."

"What?" from Plyne. And then to the waitress, who hadn't moved, "That's right, stay there. You got more comin'."

"No," Eddie said. "Listen, Wally—"

"To you?" The bouncer ripped out a laugh. He pulled his arm free from Eddie's grasp. "Move, clown. Get outa the way."

Eddie stood there.

"I said move," Plyne barked. "Get back where you belong." He pointed to the piano.

"If you'll leave her alone," Eddie said.

Again Plyne turned to the crowd. "You hear that? Can you believe it? I tell him to move and he won't move. This can't be Eddie."

From someone in the crowd, "It's Eddie, all right."

And from another, "He's still there, Hugger."

Plyne stepped back and looked Eddie up and down. He said, "What goes with you? You really know what you're doin'?"

Eddie spoke again to the waitress. "Take off, will you? Go on, fade."

"Not from this deal," the waitress said. "I like this deal."

"Sure she likes it," Plyne said. "What she got was only a taste. Now I'm gonna give her—"

"No you won't." Eddie's voice was soft, almost a whisper.

"I won't?" The bouncer mimicked Eddie's tone. "What's gonna stop me?"

Eddie didn't say anything.

Plyne laughed again. He reached out and lightly patted Eddie's head, and then he said kindly, almost paternally, "You're way outa your groove. Somebody musta been feedin' you weeds, or maybe a joker put a capsule in your coffee."

"He ain't high, Hugger," came from someone in the crowd. "He's got both feet on the floor."

From another observer, "He'll have his head on the floor if he don't get outa the way."

"He'll get outa the way," Plyne said. "All I hafta do is snap my fingers—"

Eddie spoke with his eyes. His eyes said to the bouncer, It's gonna take more than that.

Plyne read it, checked it, and decided to test it. He moved toward the waitress. Eddie moved with him, staying in his path. Someone yelled, "Watch out, Eddie—"

The bouncer swiped at him, as though swiping at a fly. He ducked, and the bouncer lunged past him, aiming a fist at the waitress. Eddie pivoted and swung and his right hand made contact with Plyne's head.

"What?" Plyne said heavily. He turned and looked at Eddie.

Eddie was braced, his legs wide apart, his hands low.

"You did that?" Plyne asked.

Did I? Eddie asked himself. Was it really me? Yes, it was. But that can't be. I'm Eddie. Eddie wouldn't do that. The man who would do that is a long-gone drifter, the wild man whose favorite drink was his own blood, whose favorite meat was the Hell's Kitchen maulers, the Bowery sluggers, the Greenpoint uglies. And that was in another city, another world. In this world it's Eddie, who sits at the piano and makes the music and keeps his tongue in his cheek. Then why—

The bouncer moved in and hauled off with his left hand,

his right cocked to follow through. As the bouncer swung, Eddie came in low and shot a short right to the belly. Plyne grunted and bent over. Eddie stepped back, then smashed a chopping left to the head.

Plyne went down.

The crowd was silent. The only sound in the Hut was the heavy breathing of the bouncer, who knelt on one knee and shook his head very slowly.

Then someone said, "I'm gonna buy new glasses. I just ain't seein' right."

"You saw what I saw," another said. "It was Eddie did that."

"I'm tellin' ya that can't be Eddie. The way he moved— that's something I ain't seen for years. Not since Henry Armstrong."

"Or Terry McGovern," one of the oldsters remarked.

"That's right, McGovern. That was a McGovern left hand, sure enough."

Then they were quiet again. The bouncer was getting up. He got up very slowly and looked at the crowd. They backed away. On the outer fringe they were pushing chairs and tables aside. "That's right," the bouncer said quietly. "Gimme plenty of room."

Then he turned and looked at the piano man.

"I don't want this," Eddie said. "Let's end it, Wally."

"Sure," the bouncer said. "It's gonna be finished in a jiffy."

Eddie gestured toward the waitress, who had moved toward the far side of the bar. "If you'll only leave her alone—"

"For now," the bouncer agreed. "Now it's you I want."

Plyne rushed to him.

Eddie met him with a whizzing right hand to the mouth. Plyne fell back, started forward, and walked into another right hand that landed on the cheekbone. Then Plyne tried to reach him with both arms flailing and Eddie went very low, grinning widely and happily, coming in to uppercut the bouncer with his left, to follow with a short right that made a crunching sound as it hit the damaged cheekbone. Plyne stepped back again, then came in weaving, some- what cautiously.

The caution didn't help. Plyne took a right to the head, three lefts to the left eye, and a straight right to the mouth. The bouncer opened his mouth and two teeth fell out.

"Holy Saint Peter!" someone gasped.

Plyne was very careful now. He feinted a left, drew Eddie in, crossed a right that missed and took a series of lefts to the head. He shook them off, drew Eddie in again with another feinting left, then crossed the right. This time it landed. It caught Eddie on the jaw and he went flying. He hit the floor flat on his back. For a few moments his eyes were closed. He heard someone saying, "Get some water—" He opened his eyes. He grinned up at the bouncer.

The bouncer grinned back at him. "How we doin'?"

"We're doin' fine," Eddie said. He got up. The bouncer walked in fast and hit him on the jaw and Eddie went down again. He pulled himself up very slowly, still grinning. He raised his fists, but Plyne was in close and pushed him back. Plyne measured him with a long left, set him up against a table and then hit him with a right that sent him over the table, his legs above his head. He hit the floor and rolled over and got up.

Plyne had circled the table and was waiting for him. Plyne chopped a right to his head, hooked a left to his ribs, then hauled off and swung a roundhouse that caught him on the side of the head. He went to his knees.

"Stay there," someone yelled at him. "For Christ's sake, stay there."

"He won't do that," the bouncer said. "You watch and see. He's gonna get up again."

"Stay there, Eddie—"

"Why should he stay there?" the bouncer asked. "Look at him grinnin'. He's havin' fun."

"Lotsa fun," Eddie said. And then he came up very fast and slugged the bouncer in the mouth, in the cut eye, and in the mouth again. Plyne screamed with agony as his eye was cut again, deeply.

The crowd was backed up against a wall. They saw the bouncer reel from a smashing blow on the mouth. They saw the smaller man lunge and hit the bouncer in the belly. Plyne was wheezing, doubled up, trying to go down. The smaller man came in with a right hand that straightened

Plyne. Then he delivered a whistling left that made a sickening sound as it hit the badly damaged eye.

Plyne screamed.

There was another scream and it came from a woman in the crowd.

A man yelled, "Someone stop it—"

Plyne took another left hook to the bad eye, then a sizzling right to the mouth, a left to the eye again, a right to the bruised cheekbone, and two more rights to the same cheekbone. Eddie fractured the bouncer's cheekbone, closed the eye and knocked four teeth from the bleeding gums. The bouncer opened his mouth to scream again and was hit with a right to the jaw. He crashed into a chair and the chair fell apart. He reached out blindly, his chin on the floor, and his hand closed on a length of splintered wood, the leg from the broken chair. As he got up, he was swinging the club with all his might at the smaller man's head.

The club hit empty air. Plyne swung again and missed. The smaller man was backing away. The bouncer advanced slowly then lunged and swung and the club grazed the smaller man's shoulder.

Eddie kept backing away. He bumped into a table and threw himself aside as the bouncer aimed again for his skull. The splintered cudgel missed his temple by only a few inches.

Too close, Eddie told himself. Much too close for health and welfare. That thing connects, you're on the critical list. Did you say critical? The shape you're in now, it's critical already. How come you're still on your feet? Look at him. He's gone sheer off his rocker, and that ain't no guess, it ain't no theory. Just look at his eyes. Or make it the one eye, the other's a mess. Look at the one eye that's open. You see what's in that eye? It's slaughter. He's out for slaughter, and you gotta do something.

Whatever it is, you better do it fast. We're in the home stretch now. It's gettin' close to the finish line. Yeah—he nearly got you that time. Another inch or so and that woulda been it. God damn these tables. All these tables in the way. But the door, the back door, I think you're near enough to make a try for it. Sure, that's the only thing you can do. That is, if you wanna get outa here alive.

He turned and made a dash toward the back door. As he neared the door, he heard a loud gasp from the crowd. He whirled, and looked, and saw the bouncer heading toward the waitress.

She was backed up against the bar. She was cornered there, blocked off. On one side it was the overturned tables. On the other side it was the crowd. The bouncer moved forward very slowly, his shoulders hunched, the cudgel raised. A low gurgling noise mixed with the blood dripping from his mouth. It was a macabre noise, like a dirge.

There was a distance of some twenty feet between the bouncer and the waitress. Then it was fifteen feet. The bouncer stepped over a fallen chair, hunched lower now. He reached out to push aside an overturned table. At that moment, Eddie moved.

The crowd saw Eddie running toward the bar, then vaulting over its wooden surface, then was hurling himself toward the food counter at the other end of the bar. They saw him arriving at the food counter and grabbing a bread knife.

He came out from behind the bar and moved between the waitress and the bouncer. It was a large knife. It had a stainless-steel blade and it was very sharp. He thought, The bouncer knows how sharp it is, he's seen Harriet cutting bread with it, cutting meat. I think he'll drop that club now and come to his senses. Look, he's stopped, he's just standing there. If he'll only drop that club.

"Drop it, Wally."

Plyne held onto the cudgel. He stared at the knife, then at the waitress, then at the knife again.

"Drop that stick," Eddie said. He took a slow step forward.

Plyne retreated a few feet. Then he stopped and glanced around, sort of wonderingly. Then he looked at the waitress. He made the gurgling noise again.

Eddie took another step forward. He raised the knife a little. He kicked at the overturned table, clearing the space between himself and the bouncer.

He showed his teeth to the bouncer. He said, "All right, I gave you a chance—"

There was a shriek from a woman in the crowd. It was

Harriet. She shrieked again as Eddie kept moving slowly toward the bouncer. She yelled, "No Eddie—please!"

He wanted to look at Harriet, to tell her with his eyes, It's all right, I'm only bluffing. And he thought, You can't do that. You gotta keep your eyes on this one here. Gotta push him with your eyes, push him back—

Plyne was retreating again. He still held the cudgel, but now his grip on it was loose. He didn't seem to realize he had it in his hand. He took a few more backward steps. Then his head turned and he was looking at the back door.

I think it's working, Eddie told himself. If I can get him outa here, get him running so's he'll be out that door and outa the Hut, away from the waitress—

Look, now, he's dropped the club. All right, that's fine. You're doing fine, Hugger. I think you're gonna make it. Come on, Hugger, work with me. No, don't look at her. Look at me, look at the knife. It's such a sharp knife, Hugger. You wanna get away from it? All you gotta do is go for that door. Please, Wally, go for that door. I'll help you get through, I'll be right with you, right behind you—

He raised the knife higher. He moved in closer and faked a slash at the bouncer's throat.

Plyne turned and ran toward the back door.

Eddie went after him.

"No—" from Harriet.

And from others in the crowd, "No, Eddie. Eddie—"

He chased Plyne through the back rooms of the Hut, through the door leading to the alley. Plyne was going very fast along the wind-whipped, snow-covered alley. Gotta stay with him, Eddie thought, gotta stay with the Hugger who needs a friend now, who sure as hell needs a chummy hand on his shoulder, a soft voice saying, It's all right, Wally. It's all right.

Plyne looked back and saw him coming with the knife. Plyne ran faster. It was a very long alley and Plyne was running against the wind. He'll hafta stop soon, Eddie thought. He's carryin' a lot of weight and a lot of damage and he just can't keep up that pace. And you, you're weighted down yourself. It's a good thing you ain't wearin' your overcoat. Or maybe it ain't so good, because I'll tell you something, bud. It's cold out here.

The bouncer was halfway down the alley, turning again, and looking, then going sideways and bumping into the wooden boards of a high fence. He tried to climb the fence and couldn't obtain a foothold. He went on running down the alley. He slipped in the snow, went down, got up, took another look back, and was running again. He covered another thirty yards and stopped once more, and then he tried a fence door. It was open and he went through.

Eddie ran up to the door. It was still open. It gave way to the small backyard of a two-story dwelling. As he entered the backyard, he saw Plyne trying to climb the wall of the house.

Plyne was clawing at the wall, trying to insert his fingers through the tiny gaps between red bricks. It was as though Plyne meant to get up the wall, even if he had to scrape all the flesh off his fingers.

"Wally—"

The bouncer went on trying to climb the wall.

"Wally, listen—"

Plyne leaped up at the wall. His fingernails scraped against the bricks. As he came down, he sagged to his knees. He straightened, looked up along the wall, and then he turned slowly and looked at Eddie.

Eddie smiled at him and dropped the knife. It landed with a soft thud in the snow.

The bouncer stared down at the knife. It was half hidden in the snow. Plyne pointed with a quivering finger.

"The hell with it," Eddie said. He kicked the knife aside.

"You ain't gonna—?"

"Forget it, Wally."

The bouncer lifted his hand to his blood-smeared face. He wiped some blood from his mouth, looked at his red-stained fingers, then looked up at Eddie. "Forget it?" he mumbled, and began to move forward. "How can I forget it?"

Easy now, Eddie thought. Let's take it slow and easy. He went on smiling at the bouncer. He said, "We'll put it this way—I've had enough."

But Plyne kept moving forward. Plyne said, "Not yet. There's gotta be a winner—"

"You're the winner," Eddie said. "You're too big for me, that's all. You're more than I can handle."

"Don't con me," the bouncer said, his pain-battered brain somehow probing through the red haze, somehow seeing it the way it was. "They saw me running away. The bouncer getting bounced. They'll make it a joke—"

"Wally, listen—"

"They'll laugh at me," Plyne said. He was crouched now, his shoulders weaving as he moved in slowly. "I ain't gonna have that. It's one thing I just can't take. I gotta let them know—"

"They know, Wally. It ain't as if they need proof."

"—gotta let them know," Plyne said as though talking to himself. "Gotta cross off all them things she said about me. That I'm just a washed-up nothing, a slob a faker a crawling worm—"

Eddie looked down at the knife in the snow. Too late now, he thought. And much too late for words. Too late for anything. Well, you tried.

"But hear me now," the bouncer appealed to himself. "Them names she called me, it ain't so. I got only one name. I'm the Hugger—" He was sobbing, the huge shoulders shaking, the bleeding mouth twisted grotesquely. "I'm the Hugger, and they ain't gonna laugh at the Hugger."

Plyne leaped, and his massive arms swept out and in and tightened around Eddie's middle. Yes he's the Hugger, Eddie thought, feeling the tremendous crushing power of the bear hug. It felt as though his innards were getting squeezed up into his chest. He couldn't breathe, he couldn't even try to breathe. He had his mouth wide open, his head flung back, his eyes shut tightly as he took the iron-hard pressure of the bouncer's chin applied to his chest bone. He said to himself, You can't take this. Ain't a living thing can take this and live.

The bouncer had him lifted now, his feet several inches off the ground. As the pressure of the bear hug increased, Eddie swung his legs forward, as though he was trying to somersault backwards. His legs went in between the bouncer's knees, and the bouncer went forward stumbling. Then they went down, and he felt the cold wetness of the snow. The bouncer was on top of him, retaining the bear hug, the straddled knees braced hard against the snow as the massive arms applied more force.

Eddie's eyes remained shut. He tried to open them and couldn't. Then he tried to move his left arm, thinking in terms of his fingernails, telling himself it needed claws and if he could reach the bouncer's face—"

His left arm came up a few inches and fell back again in the snow. The snow felt very cold against his hand. Then something happened and he couldn't feel the coldness. You're going, he said to himself. You're passing out. As the thought swirled through the fog in his brain, he was trying with his right hand.

Trying what? he asked himself. What can you do now? His right hand moved feebly in the snow. Then his fingers touched something hard and wooden. At the very moment of contact, he knew what it was. It was the handle of the knife.

He pulled at the knife handle, saying to himself, In the arm, let him have it in the arm. And then he managed to open his eyes, his remaining strength now centered in his eyes and his fingers gripping the knife. He took aim, with the knife pointed at Plyne's left arm. Get in deep, he told himself. Get it in there so he'll really feel it and he'll hafta let go.

The knife came up. Plyne didn't see it coming. At that instant Plyne shifted his position to exert more pressure with the bear hug. Shifting from right to left, Plyne took the blade in his chest. The blade went in very deep.

"What?" Plyne said. "Whatcha do to me?"

Eddie stared at his own hand, still gripping the handle of the knife. The bouncer seemed to be drifting away from him, going back and sideways. He saw the blade glimmering red, and then he saw the bouncer rolling and twitching in the snow.

The bouncer rolled over on his back, on his belly, then again on his back. He stayed there. His mouth opened wide and he started to take a deep breath. Some air went in and came out mixed with bubbles of pink and red and darker red. The bouncer's eyes became very large. Then the bouncer sighed and his eyes remained wide open and he was dead.

Eddie sat there in the snow and looked at the dead man. He said to himself, Who did that? Then he fell back in the snow, gasping and coughing, trying to loosen things up inside. It's so tight in there, he thought, his hands clasped to his abdomen, it's all squashed and outa commission. You feel it? You're damn right you feel it. Another thing you feel is the news coming in on the wire. That thing there in the snow, that's your work, buddy. You wanna look at it again? You wanna admire your work?

No, not now. There's other work we gotta do now. Them sounds you hear in the alley, that's the Hut regulars coming out to see what the score is. How come they waited so long? Well, they musta been scared. Or sorta paralyzed, that's more like it. But now they're in the alley. They're opening the fence doors, the doors that ain't locked. Sure, they figure we're in one of these backyards. So what you gotta do is, you gotta keep them outa this one here. You lock that door.

But wait—let's check that angle. How come you don't want them to see? They're gonna see it sooner or later. And what it amounts to, it's just one of them accidents. It ain't as if you meant to do it. You were aiming for his arm, and then he made that move, he traveled just about four or five inches going from right to left, from right to wrong. Sure, that's what happened, he moved the wrong way and it was an accident.

You say accident. What'll they say? They'll say homicide. They'll add it up and back it up with their own playback of what happened in the Hut. The way you jugged at him with the knife. The way you went after him when he took off. But hold it there, you know you were bluffing.

Sure, friend. You know. But they don't know. And that's just about the size of it, that bluffing business is the canoe without a paddle. Because that bluff was perfect, too perfect. Quite a sale you made, friend. You know Harriet bought it, they all bought it. They'll say you had homicide written all over your face.

Wanna make a forecast? I think they'll call it second-degree and that makes it five years or seven or ten or maybe more, depending on the emotional condition or the stomach condition of the people on the parole board. You willing to settle for that kinda deal? Well, frankly, no. Quite frankly, no.

You better move now. You better lock that door.

He raised himself on his elbows. He turned his head and looked at the fence door. The distance between himself and the door was somewhat difficult to estimate. There wasn't much daylight. What sun remained was blocked off by the dark-gray curtain, the curtain that was very thick up there, and even thicker down here where it was mottled white with the heavy snowfall. It reminded him again that he wasn't wearing an overcoat. He thought dazedly, stupidly, Oughtta go back and get your overcoat, you'll freeze out here.

It's colder in a cell. Nothing colder than a cell, friend.

He was crawling through the snow, pushing himself toward the fence door some fifteen feet away. Why do it this way? he asked himself. Why not get up and walk over there?

The answer is, you can't get up. You're just about done in. What you need is a warm bed in a white room and some people in white to take care of you. At least give you a shot to make the pain go away. There's so much pain. I wonder if your ribs are busted. All right, let's quit the goddam complaining. Let's keep going toward that door.

As he crawled through the snow toward the fence door, he listened to the sounds coming from the alley. The sounds were closer now. The voices mixed with the clattering of fence doors on both sides of the alley. He heard someone yelling, "Try that one—this one's locked." And another voice, "Maybe they went all the way up the alley—maybe they're out there in the street." A third voice disagreed, "No, they're in one of these backyards—they could'na hit the street that quick."

"Well, they gotta be somewhere around."

"We better call the law—"

"Keep movin' will ya? Keep tryin' them doors."

He crawled just a little faster now. It seemed to him that he hardly moved at all. His open mouth begged the air to come in. As it came in, it was more like someone shoveling hot ashes down his throat. Get there, he said to himself. For Christ's sake, get to that door and lock it. The door.

The voices were closer now. Then one of them yelled, "Hey look, the footprints—"

"What footprints? There's more than two sets of footprints."

"Let's try Spaulding Street—"

"I'm freezin' out here."

"I tell ya, we oughtta call the law—"

He heard them coming closer. He was a few feet away from the fence door. He tried to rise. He made it to his knees, tried to get up higher, and his knees gave way. He was face down in the snow. Get up, he said to himself. Get up, you loafer.

His hands pushed hard at the snow, his arms straightening, his knees gaining leverage as he labored to get up. Then he was up and falling forward, grabbing at the open fence door. His hands hit the door, closed it, and then he fastened the bolt. As it slipped into place, locking the door, he went down again.

I guess we're all right now, he thought. For a while anyway. But what about later? Well, we'll talk about that when we come to it. I mean, when we get the all-clear, when we're sure they're outa the alley. Then we'll be able to move. And go where? You got me, friend. I can't even give you a hint.

He was resting on his side, feeling the snow under his face, more snow coming down on his head, the wind cutting into his flesh and all the cold getting in there deep, chopping at his bones. He heard the voices in the alley, the footsteps, the fence doors opening and closing, although now the noise was oddly blurred as it came closer. Then the noise was directly outside the door, going past the door, and it was very blurred, it was more like far-off humming. Something like a lullaby, he thought vaguely. His eyes were closed, his head sank deeper into the pillow of snow. He floated down and out, way out.

The voice woke him up. He opened his eyes, wondering if he'd actually heard it.

"Eddie—"

It was the voice of the waitress. He could hear her footsteps in the alley, moving slowly.

He sat up, blinking. He raised his arm to shield his face from the driving wind and the snow.

"Eddie—"

That's her, all right. What's she want?

His arm came away from his face. He looked around, and up, seeing the gray sky, the heavy snowfall coming down on the roof of the dwelling, the swirling gusts falling off the roof into the backyard. Now the snow had arranged itself into a thin white blanket on the bulky thing that was still there in the backyard.

Still there, he thought. What did you expect? That it would get up and walk away?

"Eddie—"

Sorry, I can't talk to you now. I'm sorta busy here. Gotta check some items. First, time element. What time did we go to sleep? Well, I don't think we slept long. Make it about five minutes. Shoulda slept longer. Really need sleep. All right, let's go back to sleep, the other items can wait.

"Eddie—Eddie—"

Is she alone? he asked himself. It sounds that way. It's as though she's saying, It's all clear now, you can come out now.

He heard the waitress calling again. He got up very slowly and unlocked the door and pulled it open.

Footsteps came running toward the door. He stepped back, leaning heavily against the fence as she entered the backyard. She looked at him, started to say something, and then checked it. Her eyes followed in the direction of his pointing finger. She moved slowly in that direction, her face expressionless as she approached the corpse. For some moments she stood there looking down at it. Then her head turned slightly and she focused on the bloodstained knife imbedded in the snow. She turned away from the knife and the corpse, and sighed, and said, "Poor Harriet."

"Yeah," Eddie said. He was slumped against the fence. "It's a raw deal for Harriet. It's—"

He couldn't get the words out. A surge of pain brought a groan from his lips. He sagged to his knees and shook his head slowly. "It goes and it comes," he mumbled.

He heard the waitress saying, "What happened here?"

She was standing over him. He looked up. Through the throbbing pain, the fatigue pressing down on him, he managed to grin. "You'll read about it—"

"Tell me now." She knelt beside him. "I gotta know now."

"What for?" He grinned down at the snow. Then he groaned again, and the grin went away. He said, "It don't matter—"

"The hell it don't." She took hold of his shoulders. "Gimme the details. I gotta know where we stand."

"We?"

"Yeah, we. Come on now, tell me."

"What's there to tell? You can see for yourself—"

"Look at me," she said. She moved in closer as he raised his head slightly. She spoke quietly, in a clinical tone. "Try not to go under. You gotta stay with it. You gotta let me know what happened here."

"Something went wrong—"

"That's what I figured. The knife, I mean. You're not a knifer. You just wanted to scare him, to get him outa the Hut, away from me. Ain't that the way it was?"

He shrugged. "What difference—"

"Get off that," she cut in harshly. "We hafta get this straight."

He groaned again. He let out a cough. "Can't talk now."

"You gotta." She tightened her grip on his shoulders. "You gotta tell me."

He said, "It's—it's just one of them screwed-up deals. I thought I could reason with him. Nothing doing. He was too far off the track. Strictly section eight. Comes running at me, grabs me, and then I'm gettin' squeezed to jelly."

"And the knife?"

"It was on the ground. I'd tossed it aside so he'd know I wasn't out to carve him. But then he's usin' all his weight, he's got me half dead, and I reach out and there's the knife. I aimed for his arm—"

"Yes? Go on, tell me—"

"Thought if I got him in the arm, he'd let go. But just

then he's moving. He moves too fast and I can't stop it in time. It misses the arm and he gets it in the chest."

She stood up. She was frowning thoughtfully. She walked toward the fence door, then turned slowly and stood there looking at him. She said, "You wanna gamble?"

"On what?"

"On the chance they'll buy it."

"They won't buy it," he said. "They only buy evidence."

She didn't say anything. She came away from the fence door and started walking slowly in a small circle, her head down.

He lifted himself from the ground, doing it with a great deal of effort, grunting and wheezing as he came up off his knees. He leaned back against the fence and pointed toward the middle of the yard where the snow was stained red. "There it is," he said. "There's the job, and I did it. That's all they need to know."

"But it wasn't your fault."

"All right, I'll tip them off. I'll write them a letter."

"Yeah. Sure. From where?"

"I don't know yet. All I know is, I'll hafta travel."

"You're in great shape to travel."

He looked down at the snow. "Maybe I'll just dig a hole and hide."

"It ain't right," she said. "It wasn't your fault."

"Say, tell me something. Where can I buy a helicopter?"

"It was his fault. He messed it up."

"Or maybe a balloon," Eddie mumbled. "A nice big balloon to lift me over this fence and get me outa town."

"What a picnic," she said.

"Yeah. Ain't it some picnic?"

She turned her head and looked at the corpse. "You slob," she said to it. "You stupid slob."

"Don't say that."

"You slob. You idiot," talking quietly to the corpse. "Look what you went and done."

"Cut it out," Eddie said. "And for Christ's sake, get outa this yard. If they find you with me—"

"They won't," she said. She beckoned to him, and then gestured toward the fence door.

He hesitated. "Which way they go?"

"Across Spaulding Street," she said. "Then up the next alley. That's why I came back. I knew you hadda be in one of these yards."

She moved toward the fence door, and stood there waiting for him. He came forward very slowly, bent low, his hands clutching his middle.

"Can you make it?" she said.

"I don't know. I don't think so."

"Try," she said. "You gotta try."

"Take a look out there," he said. "I wanna be sure it's clear."

She leaned out past the fence door, looking up and down the alley. "It's all right," she said. "Come on."

He took a few more steps toward her. Then his knees buckled and he started to go down. She moved in quickly and caught hold of him, her hands hooking under his armpits. "Come on," she said. "Come on, now. You're doing fine."

"Yeah. Wonderful."

She held him on his feet, urging him forward, and they went out of the yard and started down the alley. He saw they were moving in the direction of the Hut. He heard her saying, "There's nobody in there now. They're all on the other side of Spaulding Street. I think we got a chance—"

"Quit saying we."

"If we can make it to the Hut—"

"Now look, it ain't we. I don't like this *we* business."

"Don't," she said. "Don't tell me that."

"I'm better off alone."

"Save it," she gritted. "That's corn for the squares."

"Look, Lena—" He made a feeble attempt to pull away from her.

She tightened her hold under his armpits. "Let's keep moving. Come on, we're getting there."

His eyes were closed. He wondered if they were standing still or walking. Or just drifting along through the snow, carried along by the wind. There was no way to be sure. You're fading again, he said to himself. And without sound he said to her, Let go, let go. Cantcha see I wanna sleep? Cantcha leave me alone? Say lady, who are you? What's your game?

"We're almost there," she said.

Almost where? What's she talking about? Where's she taking me? Some dark place, I bet. Sure, that's the dodge. Gonna get rolled. And maybe get your head busted, if it ain't busted already. But why cry the blues? Other people got troubles, too. Sure, everybody got troubles. Except the people in that place where it's always fair weather. It ain't on any map and they call it Nothingtown. I been there, and I know what it's like and I tell you, man, it was sheer delight and the pace never changed, it was you at the piano and you knew from nothing. Until this complication came along. This Complication we got here. She comes along with her face and her body and before you know it you're hooked. You tried to wriggle off but it was in deep and it was barbed. So the hooker scored and now you're in the creel and soon it's gonna be frying time. Well, it's better than freezing. It's really freezing out here. Out where? Where are we?

He was down in the snow. She pulled him up. He fell against her, fell away, went sideways across the alley and bumped into a fence. Then he was down again. She lifted him to his feet. "Damn it," she said, "come out of it." She bent over and took some snow in her hand and applied it to his face.

Who did that? he wondered. Who hit who? Who hit Cy in the eye with an Eskimo Pie? Was that you, George? Listen George, you take that attitude, it calls for a swing at your teeth.

He swung blindly, almost hit her in the face, and then he was falling again. She caught him. For a few moments he put up a tussle. Then he was slumped in her arms. She went sliding around him to get behind him, her arms tight around his chest, lifting him. "Now walk," she said. "Walk, damn you."

"Quit the shovin'," he mumbled. His eyes were closed. "Why you gotta shove me? I got legs—"

"Then use them," she commanded. She was bumping him with her knees to push him along. "Worse than a drunk," she muttered, bumping him harder as he tried to lean back against her. They went staggering along through the heavily falling snow. They went past four fence doors.

She was measuring the distance in terms of the fence doors on the left side of the alley. They were six fence doors away from the Hut when he fell again. He fell forward, flat in the snow, taking her down with him. She got up and tried to lift him and this time she couldn't do it. She stepped back and took a deep breath.

She reached inside her coat. Her hand went under her apron and came out holding the five-inch hatpin. She jabbed the long pin into the calf of his leg. Then again, deeper. He mumbled, "What's bitin' me?" and she said, "You feel it?" She used the hatpin again. He looked up at her. He said, "You havin' a good time?"

"A swell time," she said. She showed him the hatpin. "Want some more?"

"No."

"Then get up."

He made an effort to rise. She tossed the hatpin aside and helped him to his feet. They went on down the alley toward the back door of the Hut.

She managed to keep him on his legs as they entered the Hut, went through the back rooms and then, very slowly, down the cellar steps. In the cellar she half-carried him toward the high-stacked whisky and beer cases. She lowered him to the floor, then dragged him behind the wooden and cardboard boxes. He was resting on his side, mumbling incoherently. She shook his shoulder. He opened his eyes. She said, "Now listen to me," in a whisper. "You'll wait here. You won't move. You won't make a sound. That clear?"

He gave a slight nod.

"I think you'll be all right," she said. "For a while, anyway. They'll search all over the neighborhood, lookin' for you and Plyne. It figures they're gonna find Plyne. They'll try the alley again and they'll find him. Then it's the law and the law starts lookin' for you. But I don't think they'll look here. That is, unless they make a brilliant guess. So maybe there's a chance—"

"Some chance," he murmured. He was smiling wryly. "What am I gonna do, spend the winter here?"

She looked away from him. "I'm hopin' I can getcha out tonight."

"And do what? Take a walk around the block?"

"If we're lucky, we'll ride."

"On some kid's roller coaster? On a sled?"

"A car," she said. "I'll try to borrow a car—"

"From who?" he demanded. "Who's got a car?"

"My landlady." Then she looked away again.

He spoke slowly, watching her face. "You must rate awfully high with your landlady."

She didn't say anything.

He said, "What's the angle?"

"I know where she keeps the key."

"That's great," he said. "That's a great idea. Now do me a favor. Forget it."

"But listen—"

"Forget it," he said. "And thanks anyway."

Then he turned over on his side, his back to her.

"All right," she said very quietly. "You go to sleep now and I'll see you later."

"No you won't." He raised himself on his elbow. He turned his head and looked at her. "I'll make it a polite request. Don't come back."

She smiled at him.

"I mean it," he said.

She went on smiling at him. "See you later, mister."

"I told you, don't come back."

"Later," she said. She moved off toward the steps.

"I won't be here," he called after her. "I'll—"

"You'll wait for me," she said. She turned and looked at him. "You'll stay right there and wait."

He lowered his head to the cellar floor. The floor was cement and it was cold. But the air around him was warm, and the furnace was less than ten feet away. He felt the warmth settling on him as he closed his eyes. He heard her footsteps going up the cellar stairs. It was a pleasant sound that blended with the warmth. It was all very comforting, and he said to himself, She's coming back, she's coming back. Then he fell asleep.

He slept for six hours. Then her hand was on his shoulder, shaking him. He opened his eyes and sat up. He heard her whispering, "Quiet—be very quiet. There's the law upstairs."

It was black in the cellar. He couldn't even see the outline of her face. He said, "What time is it?"

"Ten-thirty, thereabouts. You had a nice sleep."

"I smell whisky."

"That's me," she said. "I had a few drinks with the law."

"They buy?"

"They never buy. They're just hangin' around the bar. The bartender's stewed and he's been givin' them freebees for hours."

"When'd they find him?"

"Just before it got dark. Some kids came out of the house to have a snowball fight. They saw him there in the yard."

"What's this?" he asked, feeling something heavy on his arm. "What we got here?"

"Your overcoat. Put it on. We're going out."

"Now?"

"Right now. We'll use the ladder and get out through the grating."

"And then what?"

"The car," she said. "I got the car."

"Look, I told you—"

"Shut up," she hissed. "Come on, now. On your feet."

She helped him as he lifted himself from the floor. He did it very slowly and carefully. He was worried he might bump against the wooden boxes, the cardboard beer cases. He murmured, "Need a match."

"I got some," she said. She struck a match. In the orange flare they looked at each other. He smiled at her. She didn't smile back. "Put it on," she said, indicating the overcoat.

He slipped into the overcoat, and followed her as she moved toward the stationary iron ladder that slanted up to the street grating. The match went out and she lit another. They were near the ladder when she stopped and turned and looked at him. She said, "Can you make it up the ladder?"

"I'll try."

"You'll make it," she said. "Hold onto me."

He moved in behind her as she started up the ladder. He held her around the waist. "Tighter," she said. She lit another match and said, "Rest your head against me—stay in close. Whatever you do, don't let go."

They went up a few rungs. They rested. A few more rungs, and they rested again. She said, "How's it going?" and he whispered, "I'm still here."

"Hold me tighter."

"That too tight?"

"No," she said. "Still tighter—like this," and she adjusted his arms around her middle. "Now lock your fingers," she told him. "Press hard against my belly."

"There?"

"Lower."

"How's that?"

"That's fine," she said. "Hold on, now. Hold me real tight."

They went on up the ladder. She lit more matches, striking them against the rusty sides of the ladder. In the glow, he looked up past her head and saw the underside of the grating. It seemed very far away.

When they were halfway up, his foot slipped off the rung. His other foot was slipping but he clung to her as tightly as he could, and managed to steady himself. Then they were climbing again.

But now it wasn't like climbing. It was more like pulling her down. That's what you're doing, he said to himself. You're pulling her down. You're just a goddam burden on her back, and this is only the start. The longer she stays with you, the worse it's gonna be. You can see it coming. You can see her getting nabbed and labeled an accessory. And then they charge her with stealing a car. What do you think they'll give her? I'll say three years, at least. Maybe five. That's a bright future for the lady. But maybe you can stop it before it happens. Maybe you can do something to get her out of this jam and send her on her way.

What can you do?

You can't talk to her, that's for sure. She'll only tell you to shut up. It's a cinch you can't argue with this one. This is one of them iron-heads. She makes up her mind to do something there ain't no way to swerve her.

Can you pull away from her? Can you let go and drop off the ladder? The noise would bring the law. Would she skip out before they come? You know she wouldn't. She'd stick with you right through to the windup. She's made of that kind of material. It's the kind of material you seldom run across. Maybe once in a lifetime you find one like this. Or no, make it twice in a lifetime. You can't forget the first. You'll never forget the first. But what we're getting now is a certain reissue, except it isn't in the memory, it's something alive. It's alive and it's her pressing against you. You're holding it very tightly. Can you ever let go?

He heard the waitress saying, "Hold on—"

Then he heard the noise of the grating. She was lifting it. She was working very quietly, coaxing it up an inch at a time. As it went up, the cold air rushed through and with it came flakes of snow, like needles against his face. Now she had the grating raised high enough for them to get through. She was squirming through the gap, taking him with her. The grating rested on her shoulders, then on her back, and then it was on his shoulders as he followed her over the edge of the opening. She held the grating higher and then they were both on their knees on the pavement and she was closing the grating.

Yellow light came drifting from the side window of the Hut, and glimmered dimly against the darkness of the street. In the glow, he saw the snow coming down, churned by the wind. It's more than just a snowstorm now, he thought. It's a blizzard.

They were on their feet and she held his wrist. They moved along, staying close to the wall of the Hut as they headed west on Fuller Street. He glanced to the side and saw the police cars parked at the curb. He counted five. There were two more parked on the other side of the street. The waitress was saying, "They're all empty. I looked before we climbed out." He said, "If one of them blueboys comes outa the Hut—" and she broke in with, "They'll stay in there. They got all that free booze." But he knew she wasn't sure about that. He knew she was saying it with her fingers crossed.

They crossed a narrow street. The blizzard came at them like a huge swinging door made of ice. They were bent low, pushing themselves against the wind. For another short block they stayed on Fuller, then there was another narrow street and she said, "We turn here."

There were several parked cars, and some old trucks. Halfway up the block there was an ancient Chevy, a pre-war model. The fenders were battered and much of the paint was chipped off. It was a two-door sedan, but as he looked at it, the impression it gave was that of sullen weary mule. A real racer, he thought, and wondered how she'd ever managed to start it. She was opening the door, motioning for him to get in.

Then he was leaning back in the front seat and she slid behind the wheel. She hit the starter. The engine gasped, tried to catch, and failed. She hit the starter again. The engine made a wheezing effort, almost caught, then faded and died. The waitress cursed quietly.

"It's cold," he said.

"It didn't gimme trouble before," she muttered. "It started up right away."

"It's much colder now."

"I'll get it started," she said.

She pressed her foot on the starter. The engine worked very hard, almost made it, then gave up.

"Maybe it's just as well," he said.

She looked at him. "Whaddya mean?"

"Even if it moves, it won't get far. They get a report on a stolen car, they work fast."

"Not on this job," she said. "On this one they won't get a report till morning, when my landlady wakes up and takes a look out the window. I made sure she was asleep before I snatched the key."

As she said it, she was pressing the starter again. The engine caught the spark, struggled to hold it, almost lost it, then idled weakly. She fed it gas and it responded. She released the brake and was reaching for the shift when two shafts of bright lights came shooting in from Fuller Street. "Get down," she hissed, as the headlights of the other car came closer. "Get your head down—"

They both ducked under the level of the windshield. He heard the engine noise of the other car, coming in closer, very close, then passing them and going away. As he raised his head, there was another sound. It was the waitress, laughing.

He looked at her inquiringly. She was laughing with genuine amusement.

"They just won't give up," she said.

"The law?"

"That wasn't the law. That was a Buick. A pale green Buick. I took a quick look—"

"You sure it was them?"

She nodded, still laughing. "The two ambassadors," she said.

"The one named Morris and—what's the other one's name?"

"Feather."

"Yeah, Feather, the little one. And Morris, the backseat driver. Feather and Morris. Incorporated."

"You think it's funny?"

"It's a scream," she said. "The way they're still mooching around—" She laughed again. "I bet they've circled this block a hundred times. I can hear them beefing about it, fussing at each other. Or maybe now they ain't even on speakin' terms."

He thought, Well, I'm glad she's able to laugh. It's good to know she can take it lightly. But the thing is, you can't take it lightly. You know there's a chance they spotted her when she raised her head. They ain't quite the goofers she thinks they are. They're professionals, you gotta remember that. You gotta remember they were out to get Turley, or let's say a step-by-step production that put them on your trail so they could find Turley, so they could find Clifton, so that finally they'd reach out and grab whatever it is they're after. Whatever it is, it's in South Jersey, in the old homestead deep in the woods. But when you called it a homestead, they gave it another name. They called it the hide-out.

That's what it is, all right. It's a hide-out, a perfect hide-out, not even listed in the post office. You mailed all your letters to a box number in that little town nine miles away. You know, I think we're seeing a certain pattern taking shape. It's sort of in the form of a circle. Like when you take off and move in a certain direction to get you far away, but somehow you're pulled around on that circle, it takes you back to where you started. Well, I guess that's the way it's gotta be. On the city's wanted list right now you're Number One. Hafta get outa the city. Make a run for the place where they'll never find you. The place is in South Jersey, deep in the woods. It's the hiding place of the Clifton-Turley combine, except now it's Clifton-Turley-Eddie, the infamous Lynn brothers.

So there it is, that's the pattern. With a musical background thrown in for good measure. It ain't the soft music now. It ain't the dreamy nothing-matters music that kept you far away from everything. This music here is the buzzing of the hornets. No two ways about that. You hear it getting louder?

It was the noise of the Chevy's engine. The car was moving now. The waitress glanced at him, as though waiting for him to say something. His mouth tightened and he stared ahead through the windshield. They were approaching Fuller Street.

He spoke quietly. "Make a right-hand turn."

"And then?"

"The bridge," he said. "The Delaware River Bridge."

"South Jersey?"

He nodded. "The woods," he said.

In Jersey, twenty miles south of Camden, the Chevy pulled into a service station. The waitress reached into her coat pocket and took out the week's salary she'd received from Harriet. She told the attendant to fill up the tank, and she bought some anti-freeze. Then she wanted skid chains. The attendant gave her a look. He wasn't happy about working on the skid chains, exposing himself to the freezing wind and the snow. "It's sure a mean night for driving," he commented. She said it sure was, but it was a nice night for selling skid chains. He gave her another look. She told him to get started with the skid chains. While he was working on the tires, the waitress went into the rest room. When she came out, she bought a pack of cigarettes from the machine. In the car, she gave a cigarette to Eddie and lit it for him. He didn't say thanks. He didn't seem to know he had a cigarette in his mouth. He was sitting up very straight and staring ahead through the windshield.

The attendant was finished with the skid chains. He was breathing hard as he came up to the car window. He cupped his hands and blew on them. He shivered, stamped his feet, and then gave the waitress an unfriendly look. He asked her if there was anything else she wanted. She said yes, she wanted him to do something about the windshield wipers. The wipers weren't giving much action, she said. The attendant looked up at the cold black sky and took a very deep breath. Then he opened the hood and began to examine the fuel pump and the lines coming off the pump and connecting with the wipers. He made an adjustment with the lines and said, "Try it now." She tried the wipers and they worked much faster than before. As she paid him, the attendant muttered, "You sure you got everything you need? Maybe you forgot something." The waitress thought it over for a moment. Then she said, "We could use a bracer." The attendant stamped his feet and shivered again and said, "Me too, lady." She looked down at the paper money in her hand, and murmured, "Got any to spare?" He shook his head somewhat hesitantly. She showed him a five-dollar bill. "Well," he said, "I got a pint bottle of something. But you might not like it. It's that homemade corn—"

"I'll take it," she said. The attendant hurried into the station shack. He came out with the bottle wrapped in some old newspaper. He handed it to the waitress and she handed it to Eddie. She paid for the liquor and the attendant put the money in his pocket and stood there at the car window, waiting for her to start the engine and drive away and go out of his life. She said, "You're welcome," and closed the car window and started the engine.

The skid chains helped considerably, as did the repaired windshield wipers. The Chevy had been averaging around twenty miles an hour. Now she wasn't worried about the skidding or running into something and she pressed harder on the gas pedal. The car did thirty and then thirty-five. It was headed south on Route 47. The wind was coming in from the southeast, from the Atlantic, and the Chevy went chugging into it sort of pugnaciously, the weary old engine giving loud and defiant back talk to the yowling blizzard. The waitress leaned low over the steering wheel, pressing harder on the gas pedal. The needle of the speedometer climbed to forty.

The waitress was feeling good. She talked to the Chevy. She said, "You wanna do fifty? Come on, you can do fifty."

"No, she can't," Eddie said. He was taking another drink from the bottle. They'd both had several drinks and the bottle was a third empty.

"I bet she can," the waitress said. The needle of the speedometer climbed toward forty-five.

"Quit that," Eddie said. "You're pushing her too much."

"She can take it. Come on, honeybunch, show him. Move, girl. That's it, move. You keep it up, you'll break a record."

"She'll break a rod, that's what she'll do," Eddie said. He said it tightly, through his teeth.

The waitress looked at him.

"Watch the road," he said. His voice was very tight and low.

"What gives with you?" the waitress asked.

"Watch the road." Now it was a growl. "Watch the goddam road."

She started to say something, held it back, and then focused her attention on the highway. Now her foot was lighter on the gas pedal, and the speed was slackened to thirty-five. It stayed at thirty-five while her hand came off the steering wheel, palm extended for the bottle. He passed it to her. She took a swig and gave it back to him.

He looked at the bottle and wondered if he could use another drink. He decided he could. He put his head back and tipped the bottle to his mouth.

As the liquor went down, he scarcely tasted it. He didn't

feel the burning in his throat, the slashing of the alcohol going down through his innards. He was taking a very big drink, unaware of how much he was swallowing.

The waitress glanced at him as he drank. She said, "For Christ's sake—"

He lowered the bottle from his mouth.

She said, "You know what you drank just then? I bet that was two double shots. Maybe three."

He didn't look at her. "You don't mind, do you?"

"No, I don't mind. Why should I mind?"

"You want some?" He offered her the bottle.

"I've had enough," she said.

He smiled tightly at the bottle. "It's good booze."

"How would you know? You ain't no drinker."

"I'll tell you something. This is very good booze."

"You getting high?"

"No," he said. "It's the other way around. That's why I like this juice here." He patted the bottle fondly. "Keeps my feet on the floor. Holds me down to the facts."

"What facts?"

"Tell you later," he said.

"Tell me now."

"Ain't ready yet. Like with cooking. Can't serve the dish until it's ready. This needs a little more cooking."

"You're cooking, all right," the waitress said. "Keep gulping that fire-water and you'll cook your brains to a frazzle."

"Don't worry about it. I can steer the brains. You just steer this car and get me where I'm going."

For some moments she was quiet. And then, "Maybe I'll have that drink, after all."

He handed her the bottle. She took a fast gulp, then quickly opened the car window and tossed the bottle out.

"Why'd you do that?"

She didn't answer. She pressed harder on the gas pedal and the speedometer went up to forty. Now there was no talk between them and they didn't look at each other. Later, at a traffic circle, she glanced at him inquiringly and he told her what road to take. They were quiet again until they approached an intersection. He told her to turn left. It brought them onto a narrow road and they stayed on it for some five miles, the car slowing as they approached a three-pronged fork of narrower roads. He told her to take the road that slanted left, veering acutely into the woods.

It was a bumpy road. There were deep chugholes and she held the Chevy down to fifteen miles per hour. The snow-drifts were high, resisting the front tires, and there were moments when it seemed the car would stall. She shifted from second gear to first, adjusting the hand throttle to maintain a steady feed of gas. The car went into a very deep chughole, labored to get up and out, came out and ploughed its way through another high snowdrift. There was a wagon path branching off on the right and he told her to take it.

They went ahead at ten miles per hour. The wagon path was very difficult. There were a great many turns and in places the line of route was almost invisible, blanketed under the snow. She was working very hard to keep the car on the path and away from the trees.

The car crawled along. For more than an hour it was on the twisting path going deep into the woods. Then abruptly the path gave way to a clearing. It was a fairly wide clearing, around seventy-five yards in diameter. The headlights beamed across the snow and revealed the very old wooden house in the center of the clearing.

"Stop the car," he said.

"We're not there yet—"

"D'ja hear me?" He spoke louder. "I said stop the car."

The Chevy was in the clearing, going toward the house. He reached down and pulled up on the hand brake. The car came to a stop thirty yards from the house.

His fingers were on the door handle. He heard the waitress saying, "What are you doing?"

He didn't reply. He was getting out of the car.

The waitress pulled him back. "Answer me—"

"We split," he said. He wasn't looking at her. "You go back to Philly."

"Look at me."

He couldn't do it. He thought, Well, the booze helped a little, but not enough. You shoulda had some more of that liquor. A lot more. Maybe if you'd finished the bottle you'd be able to handle this.

He heard himself saying, "I'll tell you how to get to the bridge. You follow the path to that fork in the road—"

"Don't gimme directions. I know the directions."

"You sure?"

"Yes," she said. "Yes. Don't worry about it."

Again he started to get out of the car, hating himself for doing it. He told himself to do it and get it over with. The quicker it was done, the better.

But it was very difficult to get out of the car.

"Well?" the waitress said quietly. "Whatcha waitin' for?"

He turned his head and looked at her. Something burned into his eyes. Without sound he was saying, I want you with me. You know I want you with me. But the way it is, it's no dice.

"Thanks for the ride," he said, and was out of the car and closing the door.

Then he stood there in the snow and the car pulled away from him and made a turn and headed back toward the path in the woods.

He moved slowly across the clearing. In the darkness he could barely see the outlines of the house. It seemed to him that the house was miles away and he'd drop before he got there. He was trudging through deep snow. The snow was still coming down and the wind sliced at him, hacking away at his face, ripping into his chest. He wondered if he ought to sit down in the snow and rest a while. Just then the beam of a flashlight hit him in the eyes.

It came from the front of the house. He heard a voice saying, "Hold it there, buddy. Just stay right where you are."

That's Clifton, he thought. Yes, that's Clifton. You know that voice. It's a cinch he's got a gun. You better do this very carefully.

He stood motionless. He raised his arms over his head. But the glare of the flashlight was too much for his eyes and he had to turn his face aside. He wondered if he was showing enough of his face to be recognized.

"It's me," he said. "It's Eddie."

"Eddie? What Eddie?"

He kept his eyes open against the glare as he showed his full face to the flashlight.

"Well, I'll be—"

"Hello, Clifton."

"For Christ's sake," the older brother said. He came in closer, holding the flashlight so that they could look at each other. Clifton was tall and very lean. He had black hair and blue eyes and he was fairly good-looking except for the scars. There were quite a few scars on the right side of his face. One of the scars was wide and deep and it ran from a point just under his eye, slanting down to his jaw. He wore a cream-colored camel's-hair overcoat with mother-of-pearl buttons. Under it he wore flannel pajamas. The pajama pants were tucked into knee-length rubber boots. Clifton was holding the flashlight in his left hand. In his right hand, resting back over his forearm, he had a sawed-off shotgun.

As they stood there, Clifton sprayed the ray of the flashlight across the clearing, spotting the path going into the woods. He murmured, "You sure you're alone? There was a car—"

"They took off."

"Who was it?"

"A friend. Just a friend."

Clifton kept aiming the flashlight across the clearing. He squinted tightly, checking the area at the edge of the woods. "I hope you weren't traced here," he said. "There's some people lookin' for me and Turley. I guess he told you about it. He said he saw you last night."

"He's here now? When'd he get back?"

"This afternoon," Clifton said. Then he chuckled softly. "Comes in all banged up, half froze, half dead, actually. Claims he hitched a few rides and then walked the rest of the way."

"Through them woods? In that storm?"

Clifton chuckled again. "You know Turley."

"Is he all right now?"

"Sure, he's fine. Fixed himself a dinner, knocked off a pint of whisky, and went to bed."

Eddie frowned slightly. "How come he fixed his own dinner? Where's Mom?"

"She left."

"Whaddya mean she left?"

"With Pop," Clifton said. He shrugged. "A few weeks ago. They just packed their things and shoved."

"Where'd they go?"

"Damned if I know," Clifton said. "We ain't heard from them." He shrugged again. And then, "Hey, I'm freezin' out here. Let's go in the house."

They walked across the snow and entered the house. Then they were in the kitchen and Clifton put a coffee pot on the stove. Eddie took off his overcoat and placed it on a chair. He pulled another chair toward the table and sat down. The chair had weak legs, loose in their sockets, and it sagged under his weight. He looked at the splintered boards of the kitchen floor, and at the chipped and broken plaster of the walls.

There was no sink in the kitchen. The light came from a kerosene lamp. He watched Clifton applying a lit match to the chunks of wood in the old-fashioned stove. No gas line here, he thought. No water pipes or electric wires in this house. Not a thing to connect it with the outside world. And that makes it foolproof. It's a hide-out, all right.

The stove was lit and Clifton came over to the table and sat down. He took out a pack of cigarettes, flicked it expertly and two cigarettes came up. Eddie took one. They smoked for a while, not saying anything. But Clifton was looking at him questioningly, waiting for him to explain his presence here.

Eddie wasn't quite ready to talk about that. For a while, for a little while anyway, he wanted to forget. He took a long drag at the cigarette and said, "Tell me about Mom and Pop. Why'd they leave?"

"Don't ask me."

"I'm asking you because you know. You were here when they went away."

Clifton leaned back in his chair, puffed at the cigarette, and didn't say anything.

"You sent them away," Eddie said.

The older brother nodded.

"You just put them out the door." Eddie snapped his fin-.ger. "Just like that."

"Not exactly," Clifton said. "I gave them some cash."

"You did? That was nice. That was sure nice of you."

Clifton smiled softly. "You think I wanted to do it?"

"The point is—"

"The point is, I hadda do it."

"Why?"

"Because I like them," Clifton said. "They're nice quiet people. This ain't no place for nice quiet people."

Eddie dragged at the cigarette.

"Another thing," Clifton said. "They ain't bullet-proof." He shifted his position in the chair, sitting sideways and crossing his legs. "Even if they were, it wouldn't help much. They're getting old and they can't take excitement like this."

Eddie glanced at the shiny black sawed-off shotgun on the floor. It rested at Clifton's feet. He looked up, above Clifton's head, to a shelf that showed a similar gun, a few smaller guns, and several boxes of ammunition.

"There's gonna be action here," Clifton said. "I was hoping it wouldn't happen, but I can feel it coming."

Eddie went on looking at the guns and ammunition on the shelf.

"Sooner or late," Clifton was saying. "Sooner or later we're gonna have visitors."

"In a Buick?" Eddie murmured. "A pale green Buick?"

Clifton winced.

"They get around," Eddie said.

Clifton reached across the table and took hold of Eddie's wrist. It wasn't a belligerent move; Clifton had to hold onto something.

Clifton was blinking hard, as though trying to focus on Eddie's face, to understand fully what Eddie was saying. "Who gets around? Who you talking about?"

"Feather and Morris."

Clifton released Eddie's wrist. For the better part of a minute it was quiet. Clifton sucked in smoke, expelled it in a blast, and gritted, "That Turley. That goddam stupid Turley."

"It wasn't Turley's fault."

"Don't gimme that. Don't cover for him. He's a nitwit from way back. There ain't been a time he hasn't screwed things up one way or another. But this deal tops it. This really tops it."

"He was in a fix—"

"He's always in a fix. You know why? He just can't do

things right, that's why." Clifton dragged again at the cigarette. "Ain't bad enough he gets them on his tail. He goofs
again and drags you into it."

Eddie shrugged. "It couldn't be helped. Just one of them
situations."

"Line it up for me," Clifton said. "How come they latched
on to you? How come you're here now? Gimme the wire on
this."

Eddie gave it to him, making it brief and simple.

"That's it," he finished. "Only thing for me to do was
come here. No other place for me to go."

Clifton was gazing off to one side and shaking his head
slowly.

"What'll it be?" Eddie asked. "Gonna let me stay?"

The other brother took a deep breath. "Damn it," he muttered to himself. "Damn it to hell."

"Yeah, I know what you mean," Eddie said. "You sure
need me here."

"Like rheumatism. You're a white-hot property. Philly
wants you, Pennsy wants you, and next thing they do is
call Washington. You crossed a state line and that makes it
federal."

"Maybe I'd better—"

"No, you won't," Clifton cut in. "You'll stay. You gotta
stay. When you're federal, you can't budge. They're too
slick. You make any move at all and they're on you like
tweezers."

"That's nice to know," Eddie murmured. He wasn't
thinking about himself. He wasn't thinking about Clifton
and Turley. His thoughts were centered on the waitress. He
was wondering if she'd make it back safely to Philly and
return the stolen car to its parking place. If it happened that
way she'd be all right. They wouldn't bother her. They'd
have no reason to question her. He kept telling himself it
would be all right, but he kept thinking about her and he
was worried she'd run into some trouble. Please don't, he
said to her. Please stay out of trouble.

He heard Clifton saying, "—sure picked a fine time to
come walking in."

He looked up. He shrugged and didn't say anything.

"It's one hell of a situation," Clifton said. "On one side

there's this certain outfit lookin' for me and Turley. On the other side it's the law, lookin' for you."

Eddie shrugged again. "Well, anyway, it's nice to be home."

"Yeah," Clifton said wryly. "We oughtta celebrate."

"It's an occasion, all right."

"It's a grief, that's what it is," Clifton said. "It's—" And then he forced it aside. He grinned and reached across the table and hit Eddie on the shoulder. "You know one thing? It's good to see you again."

"Likewise," Eddie said.

"Coffee's boiling," Clifton said. He got up and went to the stove. He came back with the filled cups and set them on the table. "What about grub?" he asked. "Want some grub?"

"No," Eddie said. "I ain't hungry."

They sat there sipping the black sugarless coffee. Clifton said, "You didn't tell me much about the dame. Gimme more on the dame."

"What dame?"

"The one that brought you here. You said she's a waitress—"

"Yeah. Where I worked. We got to know each other."

Clifton looked at him closely, waiting for him to tell more.

For a while it was quiet. They went on sipping the coffee. Then Clifton was saying something that he heard only vaguely, unable to listen attentively because of the waitress. He was looking directly at Clifton and it appeared he was paying close attention to what Clifton was saying. But in his mind he was with the waitress. He was walking with her and they were going somewhere. Then they stopped and he looked at her and told her to leave. She started to walk away. He went after her and she asked him what he wanted. He told her to get away from him. She walked away and he moved quickly and caught up with her. Then again he was telling her to take off, he didn't want her around. He stood there watching her as she departed. But he couldn't bear it and he ran after her. Now very patiently she asked him to decide what they should do. He told her to please go away.

It went on like that while Clifton was telling him about

certain events during the past few years, culminating in Turley's trip to Philadelphia, to Dock Street, with Turley trying to make connections along the wharves and piers where he'd once worked as a longshoreman. What Turley had sought was a boat ride for Clifton and himself. They needed the boat ride away from the continent, far away from the people who were looking for them.

The people who were looking for them were members of a certain unchartered and unlicensed corporation. It was a very large corporation that operated along the eastern seaboard, dealing in contraband merchandise such as smuggled perfumes from Europe, furs from Canada, and so forth. Employed by the corporation, Clifton and Turley had been assigned to the department that handled the more physical aspects of the business, the hijacking and the extortion and sometimes the moves that were necessary to eliminate competitors.

Some fourteen months ago, Clifton was saying, he'd decided that he and Turley were not receiving adequate compensation for their efforts. He'd talked it over with certain executives of the corporation and they told him there was no cause for complaint, they didn't have time to hear his complaints. They made it clear that in the future he was to keep away from the front office.

At that time the front office of the corporation was in Savannah, Georgia. They were always changing the location of the front office from one port to another, according to the good will or lack of good will between the executives and certain port authorities. In Savannah, an investigation was taking place and the top people of the corporation were preparing to leave for Boston. It was necessary to leave quickly because the investigators were making rapid strides, and so of course there was some confusion. In the midst of the confusion, Clifton and Turley resigned from the corporation. When they did it, they took something with them. They took a couple of hundred thousand dollars.

They took it from the safe in the warehouse where the front office was located. They did it very late at night, walking in quite casually and chatting with three fellow employees who were playing pinochle. When they showed guns, one of the card players made a move for his own and Turley kicked him in the groin, then hit him on the head with the gun butt sufficiently hard to finish him. The two other card players were Feather and Morris, with Morris perspiring as Turley hefted the gun to use the butt again, with Feather talking very fast and making a proposition.

Feather proposed that it would be better to do this with four than just two. With four walking out, the corporation would be faced with a serious problem. Feather made the point that tracing four men is considerably more difficult than tracing two. And also, Feather said, he and Morris were rather unhappy with the treatment they were getting from the corporation, they'd be grateful for this chance to walk out. Feather went on talking while Clifton thought it over, and while Turley used an acetylene torch to open the safe. Then Clifton decided that Feather was making sense, that it wasn't just a frantic effort to stay alive. Besides, Feather was something of a brain and from here on in it would take considerable brains, much more than Turley had. Another factor, Clifton reasoned, was the potential need for gun-handling, and in that category it would be Morris. He knew what Morris could do with a gun, with anything from a .38 to a Thompson. When the money was in the suitcase and they walked out of the warehouse, they took Feather and Morris with them.

On the road going north from Georgia to New Jersey, they traveled at fairly high speed. In Virginia they were spotted by some corporation people and there was a chase and an exchange of bullets and Morris proved himself rather useful. The other car was stopped with a front tire punctured, and, later, on a side road in Maryland, another corporation effort was blocked by Morris, leaning out the rear window to send bullets seventy yards down the road and through a windshield and into the face of the driver. There were no further difficulties with the corporation and that night they were crossing a bridge into South Jersey and Feather was handling the car very nicely. As Clifton told him what turns to make, he kept asking where they were going. Morris also asked where they were going. Clifton said they were going to a place where they could stay hidden for a while. Feather wanted to know if the place was sufficiently safe. Clifton said it was, describing the place, the fact that it was far from the nearest town, that it was very deep in the woods and extremely difficult to locate. Feather kept asking questions and presently Clifton decided there were too many questions and he told Feather to stop the car. Feather looked at him, and then threw a glance at Morris who was in the back seat with Turley. As Morris went for his gun, Turley hauled off and put a fist on his chin and knocked him out. Feather was trying to get out of the car and Clifton grabbed him and held him while Turley tagged him on the jaw, just under his ear. Then Feather and Morris were asleep in the road and the car was going away.

"—shoulda made a U-turn and came back and run over them," Clifton was saying. "Shoulda figured what would happen if I let them stay alive. The way it worked out, they musta played it slick. That Feather's a slick talker. He musta known just what to tell the corporation. I guess he said it was a strong-arm deal, that they didn' have no choice and they hadda come along for the ride. So the corporation takes them in again. Not all the way in, not yet. First they gotta find me and Turley. It's like they're on probation. They know they gotta make good to get in solid again."

Clifton lit another cigarette. He went on talking. He talked about Turley's witless maneuvering and his own mistake in allowing Turley to make the trip to Philadelphia.

"—had a feeling he'd mess things up," Clifton was saying. "But he swore he'd be careful. Kept telling me about his connections on Dock Street, all them boat captains he knew, and how easy it would be to make arrangements. Kept selling me on the idea and finally I bought it. We get in the car and I drive him to Belleville so he can catch a bus to Philly. For that one move alone I oughtta have my head examined."

Eddie was sitting there with his eyes half closed. He was still thinking about the waitress. He told himself to stop it, but he couldn't stop it.

"—so now it's no boat ride," Clifton was saying. "It's just sitting around, wondering what's gonna happen, and when. Some days we go out hunting for rabbits. That's a good one. We're worse off than the rabbits. At least they

can run. And the geese, the wild geese. Christ, how I envy
them geese.

"I'll tell you something," he went on. "It's really awful
when you can't budge. It gets to be a drag and in the morning you hate to wake up because there's just no place to go.
We used to joke about it, me and Turley. It actually gave us
a laugh. We got two hundred thousand dollars to invest
and no way to have fun with it. Not even on a broad. Some
nights I crave a broad so bad—

"It ain't no way to live, I'll tell you that. It's the same routine, day after day. Except once a week it's driving the nine
miles to Belleville, to buy food. Every time I take that ride, I
come near pissing in my pants. A car shows in the rear-
view mirror, I keep thinking that's it, that's a corporation
car and I'm spotted, they got me now. In Belleville I try to
play it cool but I swear it ain't easy. If anyone looks at me
twice, I'm ready to go for the rod. Say, that reminds me—"

Clifton got up from the table. He reached to the shelf, to
the assortment of guns, and selected a .38 revolver. He
checked it, then opened one of the ammunition boxes,
loaded the gun and handed it to Eddie. "You'll need this,"
he said. "Keep it with you. Don't ever be without it."

Eddie looked at the gun in his hand. It had no effect on
him. He slipped it under his overcoat, into the side pocket
of his jacket.

"Take it out," Clifton said.

"The gun?"

Clifton nodded. "Take it outa your pocket. Let's see you
take it out."

He reached under his overcoat, doing it slowly and indif-
ferently. Then the gun was in his hand and he showed it to
Clifton.

"Try it again," Clifton said, smiling at him. "Put it back in
and take it out."

He did it again. The gun felt heavy and he was awkward
with it. Clifton was laughing softly.

"Wanna see something?" Clifton said. "Watch me."

Clifton turned and moved toward the stove. He had his
hands at his sides. Then he stood at the stove and reached
toward the coffee pot with his right hand. As his fingers
touched the handle of the coffee pot, the yellow-tan sleeve

of his camel's-hair coat was a flash of caramel color, and almost in the same instant there was a gun in his right hand, held steady there, his finger on the trigger.

"Get the idea?" Clifton murmured.

"I guess it takes practice."

"Every day," Clifton said. "We practice at least an hour a day."

"With shooting?"

"In the woods," Clifton said. "Anything that moves. A weasel, a rat, even the mice. If they ain't showing, we use other targets. Turley throws a stone and I draw and try to hit it. Or sometimes it's tin cans. When it's tin cans it's long range. We do lotsa practicing at long range."

"Is Turley any good?"

"He's awful," Clifton said. "He can't learn."

Eddie looked down at the gun in his hand. It felt less heavy now.

"I hope you can learn," Clifton said. "You think you can?"

Eddie hefted the gun. He was remembering Burma. He said, "I guess so. I've done this before."

"That's right. I forgot. It slipped my mind. You got some medals. You get many Japs?"

"A few."

"How many?"

"Well, it was mostly with a bayonet. Except with the snipers. With the snipers I liked the forty-five."

"You want a forty-five? I got a couple here."

"No, this'll be all right."

"It better be," Clifton said. "This ain't for prizes."

"You think it's coming soon?"

"Who knows? Maybe a month from now. A year from now. Or maybe tomorrow. Who the hell knows?"

"Maybe it won't happen," Eddie said.

"It's gotta happen. It's on the schedule."

"You know, there's a chance you could be wrong," Eddie said. "This place ain't easy to find."

"They'll find it," Clifton muttered. He was staring at the window. The shade was down. He leaned across the table and lifted the shade just a little and looked out. He kept the shade up and stayed there looking out and Eddie turned to see what he was looking at. There was nothing out there except the snow-covered clearing, then the white of the trees in the woods, and then the black sky. The glow from the kitchen showed the woodshed and the privy and the car. It was a gray Packard sedan, expensive-looking, its chromium very bright where the grille showed under the snow-topped hood. Nice car, he thought, but it ain't worth a damn. It ain't armor-plated.

Clifton lowered the shade and moved away from the table. "You sure you ain't hungry?" he asked. "I can fix you something—"

"No," Eddie said. His stomach felt empty but he knew he couldn't eat anything. "I'm sorta done in," he said. "I wanna get some sleep."

Clifton picked up the sawed-off shotgun and put it under his arm, and they went out of the kitchen. In the parlor there was another kerosene lamp and it was lit, the flickering glimmer revealing a scraggly carpet, a very old sofa with some of the stuffing popped out, and two armchairs that were even older than the sofa and looked as though they'd give way if they were sat on.

There was also the piano.

Same piano, he thought, looking at the splintered upright that appeared somewhat ghostly in the dim yellow glow. The time-worn keyboard was like a set of decayed, crooked teeth, the ivory chipped off in places. He stood there looking at it, unaware that Clifton was watching him. He moved toward the keyboard and reached out to touch it. Then something pulled his hand away. His hand went under his overcoat and into the pocket of his jacket and he felt the full weight of the gun.

So what? he asked himself, coming back to now, to the sum of it. They take the piano away and they give you a gun. You wanted to make music, and the way it looks from here on in you're finished with that, finished entirely. From here on in it's this—the gun.

He took the .38 from his pocket. It came out easily, smoothly, and he hefted it efficiently.

He heard Clifton saying, "That was nice. You're catching on."

"Maybe it likes me."

"Sure it likes you," Clifton said. "It's your best friend from now on."

The gun felt secure in his hand. He fondled it. Then he put it back into his pocket and followed Clifton toward the rickety stairway. The loose boards creaked as they went up, Clifton holding the kerosene lamp. At the top of the stairs, Clifton turned and handed him the lamp and said, "Wanna wake up Turley? Let him know you're here?"

"No," Eddie said. "Let him sleep. He needs sleep."

"All right." Clifton gestured down the hall. "Use the back room. The bed's made up."

"Same bed?" Eddie murmured. "The one with the busted springs?"

Clifton gazed past him. "He remembers."

"I oughtta remember. I was born in that room."

Clifton nodded slowly. "You had that room for twelve-thirteen years."

"Fourteen," Eddie said. "I was fourteen when they took me off to Curtis."

"What Curtis?"

"The Institute," Eddie said. "The Curtis Institute of Music."

Clifton looked at him and started to say something and held it back.

He grinned at Clifton. He said, "Remember the slingshots?"

"Slingshots?"

"And the limousine. They came for me in a limousine, them people from Curtis. Then in the woods it was you and Turley, with slingshots, shooting at the car. The people didn't know who you were. One of the women, she says to me, 'Who are they?' and I say, 'The boys, ma'am? The two boys?' She says 'They ain't boys, they're wild animals.'"

"And what did you say?"

"I said, 'They're my brothers, ma'am.' So then of course she tries to smooth it over, starts talking about the Institute and what a wonderful place it is. But the stones kept hitting the car, and it was like you were telling me something. That I couldn't really get away. That it was just a matter of time. That some day I'd come back to stay."

"With the wild animals," Clifton said, smiling thinly at him.

"You knew all along?"

Clifton nodded very slowly. "You hadda come back. You're one of the same, Eddie. The same as me and Turley. It's in the blood."

That says it, Eddie thought. That nails it down for sure. Any questions? Well yes, there's one. The wildness, I mean. Where'd we get it from? We didn't get it from Mom and Pop. I guess it skipped past them. It happens that way sometimes. Skips maybe a hundred years or a couple hundred or maybe three and then it shows again. If you look way back you'll find some Lynns or Websters raising hell and running wild and hiding out the way we're hiding now. If we wanted to, we could make it a ballad. For laughs, that is. Only for laughs.

He was laughing softly as he moved past Clifton and went on down the hall to the back room. Then he was undressed and standing at the window and looking out. The snow had stopped falling. He opened the window and the wind came in, not blasting now. It was more like a slow stream. But it was still very cold. Nice when it's cold, he thought. It's good for sleeping.

He climbed into the sagging bed, slid between a torn sheet and a scraggly quilt, and put the gun under the pillow. Then he closed his eyes and started to fall asleep, but something tugged at his brain and it was happening again, he was thinking about the waitress.

Go away, he said to her. Let me sleep.

Then it was like a tunnel and she was going away in the darkness and he went after her. The tunnel was endless and he kept telling her to go away, then hearing the departing footsteps and running after her and telling her to go away. Without sound she said to him, Make up your mind, and he said, How can I? This ain't like thinking with the mind. The mind has nothing to do with it.

Please go to sleep, he told himself. But he knew it was no use trying. He opened his eyes and sat up. It was very cold in the room but he didn't feel it. The hours flowed past and he had no awareness of time, not even when the window showed gray and lighter gray and finally the lit-up gray of daylight.

At a few minutes past nine, his brothers came in and saw

him sitting there and staring at the window. He talked with them for a while and wasn't sure what the conversation was about. Their voices seemed blurred and through his half closed eyes he saw them through a curtain. Turley offered him a drink from a pint bottle and he took it and had no idea what it was. Turley said, "You wanna get up?" and he started to climb out of the bed and Clifton said, "It's early yet. Let's all go back to sleep," with Turley agreeing, saying it would be nice to sleep all day. They went out of the room and he sat there on the edge of the bed, looking at the window. He was so tired he wondered how he was able to keep his eyes open. Then later his head was on the pillow and he was trying hard to fall asleep but his eyes remained open and his thoughts kept reaching out, seeking the waitress.

Around eleven, he finally fell asleep. An hour later he opened his eyes and looked at the window. The full glare of noon sunlight, snow-reflected, came in and caused him to blink. He got out of bed and went to the window and stood there looking out. It was very sunny out there, the snow glittering white-yellow and across the clearing the trees, laced with ice, were sparkling like jeweled ornaments. Very pretty, he thought. It's very pretty in the woods in the wintertime.

There was something moving out there, something walking in the woods, coming toward the clearing. It came slowly, hesitantly, with a certain furtiveness. As it edged past the trees, approaching closer to the clearing, a shaft of sunlight found it, lit it up and identified it. He shook his head and rubbed his eyes. He looked again, and it was there. Not a vision, he thought. Not wishful thinking, either. That's real. You see it and you know it's real.

Get out there, he said to himself. Get out there fast and tell her to go away. You gotta keep her away from this house. Because it ain't a house, it's just a den for hunted animals. She stumbles in, she'll never get out. They wouldn't let her. They'd clamp her down and hold her here for security reasons. Maybe they've spotted her already, and you better take the gun. They're your own dear brothers but what we have here is a difference of opinion and you damn well better take the gun.

He was dressed now, pulling the gun from under the pillow, putting it in his jacket pocket, then slipping into the overcoat as he went out of the room. He moved quietly but hastily down the hall, then down the steps and out through the back door. The snow was high, and he churned his way through it, running fast across the clearing, toward the waitress.

She was leaning against a tree, waiting for him. As he came up, she said, "You ready?"

"For what?"

"Travel," she said. "I'm taking you back to Philly."

He frowned and blinked, his eyes flicking questions.

"You're cleared," she told him. "It's in the file. They're calling it an accident."

The frown deepened. "What're you giving me?"

"A message," she said. "From Harriet. From the crowd at the Hut, the regulars. They're regular, all right."

"They're backing me?"

"All the way."

"And the law?"

"The law bought it."

"Bought what? They don't buy hearsay evidence. This needs a witness. I don't have a witness—"

"You got three."

He stared at her.

"Three," she said. "From the Hut."

"They saw it happen?"

She smiled thinly. "Not exactly."

"You told them what to say?"

She nodded.

Then he began to see it. He saw the waitress in there pitching, first talking to Harriet, then going out to round up the others, ringing doorbells very early in the morning. He saw them all assembled at the Hut, the waitress telling them the way it was and what had to be done. Like a company commander, he thought.

"Who was it?" he asked. "Who volunteered?"

"All of them."

He took a deep breath. It quivered somewhat, going in. His throat felt thick and he couldn't talk.

"We figured three was enough," the waitress said. "More than three, it would seem sorta phony. We hadda make sure it would hold together. What we did was, we picked three with police records. For gambling, that is. They're on the list as well-known crapshooters."

"Why crapshooters?"

"To make it look honest. First thing, they hadda explain why they didn't tell the law right away. Reason is, they didn't wanna get pinched for gambling. Another thing, the way we lined it up they were upstairs, in the back room. The law wantsa know what they're doing up there, they got a perfect answer, they're having a private session with the dice."

"You briefed them on that?"

"We went over it I don't know how many times. At seven-thirty this morning I figured they were ready. So they go to the law and spill it and then they're signing the statements."

"Like what? What was the pitch?"

"The window in the back room was the angle we needed. From the window you look down on a slant and you can see that backyard."

"Close enough?"

"Just about. So the way they tell it to the law, they're on the floor shooting crap and they hear the commotion from downstairs. At first they don't pay it no mind, the dice are hot and they're betting heavy. But later it sounds bad from downstairs, and then they hear the door slamming when you chase him out to the alley. They go to the window and look out. You getting it now?"

"It checks," he nodded.

"They give it to the law like a play-by-play, exactly the way you told it to me. They said they saw you throwing the knife away and trying to talk to him but he won't listen, he's sort of off his rocker and he comes leaping in. Then he's got you in the bear hug and the way it looks, you won't come outa there alive. They said you made a grab for the knife, tried to stick him in the arm to get him off you and just then he shifts around and the blade goes into his chest."

He gazed past her. "And that's it? I'm really cleared?"

"Entirely," she said. "They dropped all charges."

"They hold the crapshooters?"

"No, just called them names. Called them goddamn liars and kicked them outa the station house. You know how it is with the law. If they can't make it stick, they drop it."

He looked at her. "How'd you get here?"

"The car."

"The Chevy?" frowning again. "Your landlady's gonna—"

"It's all right," she said. "This time it's rented. I slipped her a few bucks and she's satisfied."

"That's good to know." But he was still frowning. He turned and looked across the clearing, at the house. He was focusing on the upstairs windows. He murmured, "Where's the car?"

"Back there," she said. "In the woods. I didn't want your people to see. I thought if they spotted me, it might get complicated."

He went on looking at the house. "It's complicated already. I can't go away without telling them."

"Why not?"

"Well, after all—"

She took hold of his arm. "Come on."

"I really oughtta tell them."

"The hell with them," she said. She tugged at his arm. "Come on, will you? Let's get outa here."

"No," he murmured, still looking at the house. "First I gotta tell them."

She kept tugging at his arm. "You can't go back there. That's a hide-out. We'll both be dragged in—"

"Not you," he said. "You'll wait here."

"You'll come back?"

He turned his head and looked at her. "You know I'll come back."

She let go of his arm. He started walking across the clearing. It won't take long, he thought. I'll just tell them the way it is, and they'll understand, they'll know they got nothing to worry about, it stays a hide-out. But on the other hand, you know Clifton. You know the way he thinks, the way he operates. He's strictly a professional. A professional takes no chances. With Turley it's different. Turley's more on the easy side and you know he'll see it your way. I hope you can bring Clifton around. Not with pleading, though. Whatever you do, don't plead with him. Just let him know you're checking out with the waitress and give him assurance she'll keep her mouth shut. And what if he says no? What if he goes out and brings her into the house and says she's gotta stay? If it comes to that, we'll hafta do something. Maybe it won't come to that. Let's hope so, anyway. Let's see if we can keep it on the bright side. Sure, that's better. It's nice to think along the cheery lines, to tell yourself it's gonna work out fine and you won't be needing the gun.

He was a little more than halfway across the clearing, moving fast through the snow. He was headed toward the back door of the house, the door some sixty feet away and then fifty feet when he heard the sound of an automobile.

And even before he turned and looked, he was thinking, That ain't the Chevy going away. That's a Buick coming in.

He pivoted, his eyes aiming at the edge of the woods where the wagon path showed a pale green Buick. The car came slowly, impeded by the snow. Then it gave a lurch, the snow spraying as the tires screeched, and it was coming faster now.

They followed her, he thought. They followed her from Philly. Kept their distance so it wouldn't give them away in the rear-view mirror. Score one for them. It's quite a score, that's for sure. Maybe it's a grand slam.

He saw Feather and Morris getting out of the car. Morris circled the car and came up to Feather and they stood there talking. Morris was pointing toward the house and Feather was shaking his head. They were focused on the front of the house and he knew they hadn't seen him. But they will, he thought. You make another move and you're spotted. And this time it's no discussions, no preliminaries. This time you're on the check-off list and they'll try to put you outa the way.

What you need, of course, is a fox-hole. It would sure

come in handy right now. Or a sprinter's legs. Or better yet, a pair of wings. But I think you'll hafta settle for the snow. The snow looks deep enough.

He was crouched, then flattened on his belly in the snow. In front of his face it was a white wall. He brushed at it, his fingers creating a gap, and he looked through it and saw Feather and Morris still standing beside the car and arguing. Morris kept gesturing toward the house and Feather was shaking his head. Morris started walking toward the house and Feather pulled him back. They were talking loudly now but he couldn't make out what they were saying. He estimated they were some sixty yards away.

And you're some fifteen yards from the back door, he told himself. Wanna try it? There's a chance you can make it, but not much of a chance, considering Morris. You remember what Clifton said about Morris and his ability with a gun. I think we better wait a little longer and see what they're gonna do.

But what about her? You forgetting her? No, it ain't that, you know damn well it ain't that. It's just that you're sure she'll use her head and stay right there where she is. She stays there, she'll be all right.

Then he saw Feather and Morris taking things from the car. The things were Tommy guns. Feather and Morris moved toward the house.

But that's no way to do it, he said to them. That's like betting everything on one card, hoping to fill an inside straight. Or it could be you're too anxious, you've waited a long time and you just can't wait any more. Whatever the reason, it's a tactical error, it's actually a boner and you'll soon find out.

You sure? he asked himself. You really sure they'll come out losers? Better give it another look and line it up the way it is. I think it's Clifton and Turley in bed asleep and of course you're hoping they heard the car when it came outa the woods and they ain't asleep. But that's only hoping, and hoping ain't enough. If they're still asleep, you gotta wake them up.

You gotta do it now. Right now. After all, it's only fifteen yards to the back door. Maybe if you crawl it—No, you can't crawl it. You don't have time for that. You'll hafta run. All right let's run.

He was up and racing toward the back door. He'd made less than five yards when he heard the blast of a Tommy and saw punctures in the snow in front of him, a few feet off to the side.

Nothing doing, he told himself. You'll never make it. You'll hafta pretend you're hit. And as the thought flashed through his brain he was already going down in simulated collapse. He hit the snow and rolled over and then rested on his side, motionless.

Then he heard the other guns, the shots coming from an upstairs window. He looked up and saw Clifton, with the sawed-off shotgun. A moment later it was Turley showing at another window. Turley was using two revolvers.

He grinned and thought, Well, anyway, you did it. You managed to wake them up. They're really awake now. They're wide awake and very busy.

Feather and Morris were running back to the car. Feather seemed to be hit in the leg. He was limping. Morris turned and let go a blast at Turley's window. Turley dropped one of the revolvers and grabbed at his shoulder and ducked out of sight. Then Morris took aim at Clifton, started a volley and Clifton quickly took cover. It was all happening fast and now Feather was on his knees crawling behind the Buick to use it as a shield. Morris moved close to the house and sent another blast at the upstairs windows, swinging the Tommy to get as many bullets up there as he could. Now from the house there was no shooting at all. Morris kept blasting at the upstairs window. Feather yelled at him and he lowered the gun and walked backwards toward the Buick. He stood at the side of the Buick, the Tommy still lowered but appearing ready as he looked up at the windows.

Some moments later the back door opened and Clifton came running out. He was carrying a small black suitcase. He was running toward the gray Packard parked near the woodshed. As he neared the car, he stumbled and the suitcase fell open and some paper money dropped out. Clifton bent over to pick it up. Morris didn't see this happening. Morris was still watching the upstairs windows. Now

Clifton had the suitcase closed again and was climbing into the Packard. Then Turley, holding a sawed-off shotgun and a revolver with one hand while his other hand clutched his shoulder, came out of the back door and joined Clifton in the Packard.

The motor started and the Packard accelerated very fast, coming out from the rear of the house and sweeping in a wide circle, cutting through the snow with the skid-chained tires getting full traction, the car now moving at high speed across the clearing, aiming at the wagon path leading into the woods. Morris was using the Tommy again but he was somewhat disconcerted and his shooting was off. He shot for the tire and he was short. Then he shot for the front side window and hit the rear side window. Feather was yelling at him and he kept shooting at the Packard, now running toward the Packard as it went galloping away from him. He was screaming at the Packard, his voice cracked and twisted, with the Thompson still blasting but no longer useful because he couldn't aim it, he was much too upset.

Feather was crawling along the side of the Buick, opening the door and climbing in behind the wheel. Morris had stopped running but was still shooting at the Packard. From the Packard there was a return of fire as Turley leaned out and used the sawed-off shotgun. Morris let out a yowl and dropped the Thompson and began to hop around, his left arm dangling, his wrist and hand bright red, the redness dripping. He kept hopping around and making loud noises. Then with his right hand he pulled out a revolver and shot at the Packard as it cut across the clearing headed for the wagon path. The shot went very wide and then the Packard was on the wagon path and going away.

Feather opened the rear door of the Buick and Morris climbed in. The Buick leaped into a turn and aimed at the wagon path to chase after the Packard.

Eddie sat up. He looked to the side and saw the waitress running out from the edge of the woods. She was coming fast across the clearing and he waved at her to get back, to stay in the woods until the Buick was gone. Now the Buick had slowed just a little and he knew they'd seen the waitress.

He reached into his jacket pocket and pulled out the .38.

With his other hand he kept waving at her to get back.

The Buick came to a stop. Feather was using the Tommy, shooting at the waitress. Eddie fired blindly at the Buick, unable to aim because he wasn't thinking in terms of hitting anything. He kept pulling the trigger, hoping it would get the Tommy off the waitress. With his fourth shot he lured the Tommy to point in his direction. He felt the swish of slugs going past his head and he fired a fifth shot to keep the Tommy on him and away from her.

He couldn't see her now, he was concentrating on the Buick. The Tommy had stopped firing and the Buick was moving again. It picked up speed going toward the wagon path and he thought, It's the Packard they want, they're going away to go after the Packard. Will they get it? It really doesn't matter. You don't even want to think about it. You got her to think about. Because you can't see her now. You're looking and you can't see her.

Where is she? Did she make it back to the woods? Sure, that's what happened. She ran back and she's waiting there. So it's all right. You can go to her now. The hornets are gone and it's nice to know you can drop the gun and go to her.

He dropped the .38 and started walking through the snow. At first he walked fast, but then he slowed, and then he walked very slowly. Finally he stopped and looked at something half hidden in the deep snow.

She was resting face down. He knelt beside her and said something and she didn't answer. Then very carefully he turned her onto her side and looked at her face. There were two bullet holes in her forehead and very quickly he looked away. Then his eyes were shut tightly and he was shaking his head. There was a sound from somewhere but he didn't hear it. He didn't know he was moaning.

He stayed there for a while, kneeling beside Lena. Then he got up and walked across the clearing and went into the woods to look for the Chevy. He found it parked between some trees near the wagon path. The key was in the ignition lock and he drove the Chevy into the clearing. He placed the body in the back seat. It's gotta be delivered, he thought. It's just a package gotta be delivered.

He took her to Belleville. In Belleville the authorities held him for thirty-two hours. During that time they offered him food but he couldn't eat. There was an interval of getting into an official car with some men in plain clothes, and he guided them to the house in the woods. He was vaguely aware of answering their questions, although his answers seemed to satisfy them. When they found Tommy slugs in the clearing it confirmed what he'd told them in Belleville. But then they wanted to know more about the battle, the reason for it, and he said he couldn't tell them much about that. He said it was some kind of a dispute between these people and his brothers and he wasn't sure what it was about. They grilled him and he kept saying, "Can't help you there," and it wasn't an evasion. He really couldn't tell them because it wasn't clear in his mind. He was far away from it and it didn't matter to him, it had no importance at all.

Then, in Belleville again, they asked if he could help in establishing the identity of the victim. They said they'd done some checking but they couldn't find any relatives or records of past employment. He repeated what he'd told them previously, that she was a waitress and her first name was Lena and he didn't know her last name. They wanted to know if there was anything more. He said that was all he knew, that she'd never told him about herself. They shrugged and told him to sign a few papers, and when he'd done that, they let him go. Just before he walked out, he asked if they'd found where she lived in Philadelphia. They gave him the address of the rooming house. They were somewhat perplexed that he hadn't even known the address. After he walked out, one of them commented, "Claimed he hardly knew her. Then why's he taking it so hard? That man's been hit so hard he's goofy."

Later that day, in Philadelphia, he returned the Chevy to its owner. Then he went to his room. Without thinking about it, he pulled down the shade and then he locked the door. At the wash basin he brushed his teeth and shaved and combed his hair. It was as though he expected company and wanted to make a presentable appearance. He put on a clean shirt and a necktie and seated himself on the edge of the bed, waiting for a visitor.

He waited there a long time. At intervals he slept, pulled from sleep whenever he heard footsteps in the hall. But the footsteps never approached the door.

Very late that night there was a knock on the door. He opened the door and Clarice came in with some sandwiches and a carton of coffee. He thanked her and said he wasn't hungry. She unwrapped the sandwiches and forced them into his hands. She sat there and watched him while he ate. The food had no taste but he managed to eat it, washing it down with the coffee. Then she gave him a cigarette, lit one for herself, and after taking a few puffs she suggested they go out for a walk. She said the air would do him good.

He shook his head.

She told him to get some sleep and then she went out of the room. The next day she was there again with more food. For several days she kept bringing him food and urging him to eat. On the fifth day he was able to eat without being coaxed. But he refused to go out of the room. Each night she asked him to go for a walk and told him he needed fresh air and some exercise and he shook his head. His lips smiled at her, but with his eyes he was begging her to leave him alone.

Night after night she kept asking him to go for a walk. Then it was the ninth night and instead of shaking his head, he shrugged, put on his overcoat and they went out.

They were on the street and walking slowly and he had no idea where they were going. But suddenly, through the darkness, he saw the orange glow of the lit-up sign with some of the bulbs missing.

He stopped. He said, "Not there. We ain't going there."

"Why not?"

"Nothing there for me," he said. "Nothing I can do there."

Clarice took hold of his arm. She pulled him along toward the lit-up sign.

Then they were walking into the Hut. The place was jammed. Every table was taken and they were three-deep and four-deep all along the bar. It was the same crowd, the same noisy regulars, except that now there was very little noise. Just a low murmuring.

He wondered why it was so quiet in the Hut. Then he saw Harriet behind the bar. She was looking directly at him. Her face was expressionless.

Now heads were turning and others were looking at him and he told himself to get out of here, get out fast. But Clarice had tightened her hold on his arm. She was pulling him forward, taking him past the tables and toward the piano.

"No," he said. "I can't—"

"The hell you can't," Clarice said, and kept pulling him toward the piano.

She pushed him onto the revolving stool. He sat there staring at the keyboard.

And then, from Harriet, "Come on, give us a tune."

But I can't, he said without sound. Just can't.

"Play it," Harriet yelled at him. "Whatcha think I'm payin' you for? We wanna hear some music."

From the bar someone shouted, "Do it, Eddie. Hit them keys. Put some life in this joint."

Others chimed in, coaxing him to get started.

He heard Clarice saying, "Give, man. You got an audience."

And they're waiting, he thought. They've been coming here every night and waiting.

But there's nothing you can give them. You just don't have it to give.

His eyes were closed. A whisper came from somewhere, saying, You can try. The least you can do is try.

Then he heard the sound. It was warm and sweet and it came from a piano. That's fine piano, he thought. Who's playing that?

He opened his eyes. He saw his fingers caressing the keyboard.

About the Author

David Goodis was born in Philadelphia in 1917. The publication of *Dark Passage* in 1946 established him as a leading author of crime fiction and after the success of the film, starring Humphrey Bogart and Lauren Bacall, he joined the Warner Brothers payroll as a screen writer. His collaboration with Hollywood was less than ideal and in 1950 he returned to Philadelphia and continued to write crime fiction until his death in 1967.

·